The Odious Child

The Odious Child

Carolyn Black

NIGHTWOOD EDITIONS

1 2 3 4 — 14 13 12 11

Nightwood Editions
P.O. Box 1779
Gibsons, BC V0N 1V0
Canada
www.nightwoodeditions.com

Cover illustration and design by Jana Curll
Printed and bound in Canada

This book has been produced on 100% post-consumer recycled, ancient-forest-free paper, processed chlorine-free and printed with vegetable-based dyes.

Nightwood Editions acknowledges financial support from the Government of Canada through the Canada Book Fund and the Canada Council for the Arts, and from the Province of British Columbia through the BC Arts Council and the Book Publishing Tax Credit.

Library and Archives Canada Cataloguing in Publication

Black, Carolyn, 1974–
The odious child / Carolyn Black.

Short stories.
ISBN 978-0-88971-254-6

I. Title.

PS8603.L245O45   2011 C813'.6   C2011-900043-1

For my family
and those who love order

Contents

At World's End, Falling Off

For his beauty, I would have crouched at his feet and shrieked like a jackal.

I avoid beautiful men normally, for I am not beautiful. As a rule, I favour the style of man who will date me, the style of man who hovers in corners at parties, looking nervous, or cultivates off-putting habits, like cleaning his ears in public. Three years ago, I went out with a man who would open up sugar packets in restaurants, empty the sugar onto the table, lick his finger, dip it into the puddle of spilled sugar, then lick the sugar off his finger. Again and again. Lick. Dip. Lick. Dip. Even if he was eating with new acquaintances he would do this. Lick. Dip. Lick. Dip. Needless to say, he was not beautiful.

I ended that relationship and time passed.

I began pursuing couples through the galleries of the ceramics museum where I work. Among the eighteenth-century tureens from Chelsea, part of our permanent collection, I cornered a man and woman. They had stopped in front of a display case that held a soup tureen shaped like a rabbit. They stood on one side and I stood on the other, squinting at them through the glass. Their hands met and joined. I rarely stand still, but at that moment, I wanted to root down and begin a secure lifetime with somebody else.

So I bought the beautiful man from a matchmaking website.

The men using the site had been kind enough to explain themselves — their heights, ages, desires and goals — in under one hundred words. These words appeared beside their photos. I could imagine sorting these men into a stack with a rubber band around it. I could imagine collecting and trading these men with co-workers. In fact, the photos with their corresponding blocks of description reminded me of the museum — the men looked like artifacts on display.

This was comforting.

Human existence, it seems to me, is a forlorn clutching after short-lived things. Artifacts remain in cases, unchanged year after year; so much else just slides from my hands.

Here is where I should say what I do at the museum. I set up display cases and write the descriptive cards that will be mounted on the cases or on the walls beside them. I write the cards using the fewest sentences possible. These sentences contain short, simple words. I pile the simple words on top of each other — like beads on a string or pennies in a roll or fetishes hoarded in a cabinet — and connect them with a series of coordinating conjunctions (ideally "and" and "and" and "and"; ideally not subordinating conjunctions like "unless" or "although," which demand more complex turns of thought and a backward hiccup in logic). The logic must surge forward, as it does when a child tells a story. I do not want our patrons bored. They like to move quickly from one item to the next, without pausing or pondering. Luckily, even complex thoughts can be expressed with simple words and logic. I believe that to be true.

For instance, I might write, "The vessel is the oldest ceramic form used today, and some of its uses include serving food, drinking, storing items and decorating." I would never write, "Although problematic, three broad categories of functional, sculptural and conceptual can be identified; however, a functional piece can still be sculptural in its form and conceptual in its intent." The woman I replaced wrote sentences like, "Human folly in all its manifestations is never far below the surface of these painted scenes." She was asked, gently, to leave.

I believe in what I do and why I do it. Sometimes, though, when I write a card that surges forward in a short burst and then stops, it does not remind me of a story told by a child, but the noise an adult might make at world's end, falling off.

Anyway. I posted a blurry photo of myself on the dating website, stated that my age was thirty-nine, and invented a nickname, for members of the site did not use their true names. The important thing about my photo was the setting – a park with tall trees and inviting grass. I called myself "Country Wife," after the William Wycherley play. The play is over three hundred years old, but I thought the name hinted at my simplicity and sweetness. I do not posses either of these wifely virtues although I felt that I might with the right accessories. Perhaps a sundress. Perhaps a necklace made from shells. The name did not hint at my jealous rages or need for fastidious hygiene in lovers. I was climbing into a box, the Country Wife box, and if I did not follow through, if I slipped out of the box for even a minute, anyone who chose me would have just cause to complain. Then I saw the beautiful man's photo and stopped worrying.

His nickname was "Happiness."

I'd mention his true name, but that would slow me down. A name calls up a whole host of individual traits. These traits change and multiply the longer you know someone, and they multiply in confusing and contradictory ways. His photo is what I noticed, long before I learned his name. His photo made my eyes moist and my pelvic floor tighten. He looked like the actor on that commercial for life insurance – the same square jaw, the same thick brown hair, cut short except for a ledge of bang jutting over his forehead. Under his low brow were deep-set brown eyes and tawny skin and a full mouth, like a woman's except for the tuft of hair under his lower lip. In this beautiful face lay a kind of blankness, a lack of commitment to any one expression. I could write on this face whatever I wanted.

I paid ten dollars to send him an email. True, I had

never dated a beautiful man, but I had never used my credit card to meet one either. As I punched in numbers on the computer keyboard, gawking at his picture, anything seemed possible.

A few days later, we met outside the movie theatre. He wore a turquoise suede jacket and three silver rings on the fingers of one hand. He stood before a movie poster, one hand on his hip, his head tilted back. The poster showed a sunny porch filled with baskets of apples. When I approached, without turning his head he said, "Simple things make me happy." He had written this same sentence as part of his one hundred words, and I liked it because I thought it matched my Country Wife ambitions of hearth and home.

"Simple things make me happy," he said now, but he squinted at the poster as though it were every minute receding from him. In those minutes, with his low brow, his soft mouth pinched at the corners and a tic in his jawbone, he looked neither simple nor happy but miserable in the most complex of ways. Right then, I could have confessed my own desire for a happiness that never came, but I did not, because right then I felt angry. I hoped I had not been a victim of false advertising. He had promised happiness as though he already possessed it, as though it were on offer for any woman to acquire, with him. I wanted to stamp my foot and shout, "This was not disclosed in your profile!" I wanted to file a report with some consumers' tribunal. In my vision of the beautiful man, he spoke smiling gallantries and looked only at the woman beside him. But now when he turned from the poster to look at me, he was not smiling, and his eyes widened in surprise, as though he had just woken up and found himself in a movie theatre. Furrows ran across his forehead like deep riverbeds of woe. Tragedy had washed over him for years, I imagined, and his life was a struggle and a struggle and a struggle.

Then he smiled shyly, lowering his chin and looking up at me from under raised and bushy eyebrows. I love men who look up at me from under their eyebrows because I feel it implies a gentle nature. He spoke my name softly and did indeed move towards me with a yielding grace. I was beside myself with wonder. I had never been close to a beautiful man before and now one was meeting me at the movies. He was so beautiful that, when he smiled, people with their backs to us turned around and stared. That's how beautiful he was.

And was I beautiful? I had worked hard. I had maxed out my credit card. Under my parka, I wore a new white peasant blouse and a necklace of wooden beads and wooden hoop earrings to match. I had tousled my hair with an expensive mousse so it fell down my back in loose, unbrushed waves. I had bought makeup in light beige and pink to look as though I was not wearing any makeup. But I was. It had taken an hour to apply. My nose was still too pendulous, and my lips too thin, my smile too gummy. I was not beautiful, but I was passable and wearing the right accessories. Perhaps he could see beyond me, the awkward woman standing in front of him, to the vision my profile had promised.

Otherwise, I had already made up my mind about who he was and the kind of life we could lead together, and as I picked out candy at the snack bar, everything I thought I heard him say rang with the import of the future. He told me that he managed a small bookstore, and I delighted in this news because our both working in the arts meant we shared something and some day, when we both had time, we could sit down and talk about Art and Ideas. But mostly everything was a blur except my vision of him standing beside me in life through thick and thin, and dandling our children on his beautiful knees. I could not see further or deeper and did not have time to try. Right then, we had to get on with the business of courtship.

We took our seats, the lights dimmed, and I hoped we were about to see a movie where a loving couple gets everything they always wanted.

The movie started. It was a movie about the climate crisis. The beautiful man looked at me from the corner of his eye, furrowing his brow, and I suspected that he was tired of being a beautiful man and wanted to be a different style of man altogether, one who was concerned about the climate crisis — he had suggested the movie and now readjusted the collar on his suede jacket as though embarrassed to be wearing such an opulent material. Up on the screen, a dull, non-beautiful man was speaking about how much extra carbon dioxide filled the air and what this meant for the weather. Scenes of New Orleans after Hurricane Katrina came on the screen. People who had lost their families and homes stood in the flood water and cried and raised their arms skyward. The beautiful man took his arm from the armrest between us and leaned away from me. He started twisting one of his rings around his finger, around and around, and then just covered over his ring fingers with his other, naked, hand.

The dull man went on about how floods would soon bury immense tracts of land and create millions of climate refugees. I thought of all those displaced persons, the dispossessed, and how crowded the remaining land would be with us and all our things. Wouldn't we suffocate crowded together, trying to breathe air filled with extra carbon dioxide? Panicking, I looked at the beautiful man. With his rings, turquoise jacket and cultivated patch of hair under his lip, shaved just so, he no longer looked like a human being . . .

He looked like surplus goods, cluttering up the earth.

Right then, something fathomless happened in that movie theatre.

Right then, some vast, unknowable thing put its mouth to mine and kissed me.

Then it inhaled.

It inhaled with a gulp, and a cold slithering came up and out of me, leaving a chilly hollow in my abdomen.

Shivering, I squeezed the beautiful man's arm.

"We have to go. We have to get out of here."

I do not like to think about sickness or speak about sickness. My father lies dying in our basement apartment, as he has for the past three years, and I can do nothing for him except the tedious, daily routines of caretaking and sorrow. The dying could be finished tomorrow or it could be finished in two years from now. The doctors do not know. His dying, the deterioration of his body, represents a big portion of my life that only bears thinking about when I am in it. Otherwise, I do not think or talk about sickness. That is why I left the movie theatre.

We walked out of the theatre, me ignoring that feeling in my belly I could not make sense of. I had eaten too many licorice nibs, that was it. As for the vast, unknowable thing . . . a mind irritated by indigestion plays strange tricks. I did not feel uncomfortably full though. I felt empty.

I tried to think about the movie instead and how it was not a good piece of art but, rather, a PowerPoint presentation by a dull speaker. It was not the most dramatic way to present the facts, but as the facts seemed indisputable and dire, how trivial to point out that the movie was not a good piece of art.

"It was not a good piece of art," I said anyway.

The beautiful man's mouth pursed as though he were sucking back some words he wanted to say.

Looking at his fretful mouth, I guessed that even though he was beautiful he was picked on in high school — shoved against lockers and in the boys' change room, with his feminine and docile manner, probably worse. Standing beside me he was only an inch taller, not a large man at all, more like a girl than a husband. I looked away.

Still, he insisted on speaking, on saying the most

ready-made of remarks, "I thought the movie was powerful . . ."

Then softly, " . . .what we saw of it."

To save the evening, desperate measures were required, but after all, these were desperate times.

"I will show you where I work," I said. "I will show you some real art," for I had the keys to the museum and the pass code to deactivate the alarm. I also hoped that being in a familiar environment would calm my stomach.

I took his hand and pulled him along the street, a few blocks to the museum. We went in silence to the side door, through the staff entrance, and into the galleries, where we walked past Chinese porcelain and English pottery, earthenware plates and stoneware vases, teapots, bowls, chargers and porringers, tankards, mustard pots, tobacco jars and pedestal jars, fuddling cups and chocolate cups and ewers and snuff boxes and confectionary dishes and figurines and scent bottles. We walked without stopping, past all my labels, too. "Mug with a wagon, a man and a horse," "Posset pot with Chinese figure in garden," "Dish with scene symbolizing fecundity," "Dish portraying the Crucifixion of Christ." We walked past without stopping, through one gallery after another, not at all like the couple I had seen standing still beside the rabbit tureen.

Then he did stop. He asked, "Were any of these things ever used?"

"Some were. Some were just for looking at. Now they are all just for looking at."

He started to pull down his eyebrows and send the lines across his forehead.

There was no more time for talking; I decided. I took him through a locked door and down some stairs into Collection Room A.

Collection Room A is a massive concrete room, the length of two gymnasiums, with shelves of ceramics and boxes packed with ceramics. The shelves stretch as high as the twenty-four-foot ceiling. Every day we pull small boxes down and replace them with larger boxes. Soon there will be no room left, but nobody talks about this. We just pack the boxes tighter. The same is true of Collection Rooms B, C and D.

I pulled the beautiful man between the two shelves farthest from the white emergency light above the door, and we walked to where they ended at the concrete wall.

He leaned back against the wall, eyes lowered, head turned, as though he were posing in a magazine. I leaned myself against him and kissed him on the mouth. He kept his head turned, not looking at me, but letting me look at him, for that's how it works. If one person is looking, the other person does not often do the looking in return.

We kissed for a long time. Most men treat my body as though it were a machine with buttons. The harder they work the buttons, the more I know they want from the machine. The beautiful man did not work my buttons at all, but merely stood against the wall and let me look at him and kiss him.

Then he tugged on his fly and pulled down the front of

his pants, while holding up the tails of his shirt. I could not believe how beautiful he was against the concrete. In those monochromes of the dark – the varying shades of blue and grey and black – his skin glowed. Dark hair, light skin, dark clothes. His eyelids were white, and his mouth was black. He looked like a sculpture, a part of the concrete, and at his waist, through his shirttails and zipper, the thrust of his penis. He did not put out his hand to touch me, to take anything or try to give it. He said only, "Please, please."

I put my hand on him, but it was not enough, he was so beautiful. I knelt on the stone floor and put my mouth around him, but it was not enough, he was so beautiful. I pulled him down and gently lay him on his back on the concrete, with my hand under his head, and he tucked his face into my neck and disappeared into me, and it was almost enough.

He was so beautiful.

I think I said things then about how beautiful he was and how I adored him. I said them over and over so they would become true and lasting, but before I had time to say everything, I was finished and then he was finished.

We got up and set out back the way we came between the shelves. He did not kiss me or take my hand, only looked at me shyly from under his eyebrows. I felt wetness between my legs but not much. I could not even tell if it was mine or his, there was so little. I know I should say that we used a condom, but I had decided that since he would be my husband some day whatever happened would happen, and what could one do?

As I reset the museum's alarm, my indigestion returned, worse than before. Perhaps I was not full, but hungry. That made more sense. That explained the cold hollow in my belly.

"Let's go grab some food," I said.

We left the museum and walked out into the broad world.

On the steps of the museum, a man slept, wearing a torn rag of a t-shirt. His arms and hands were bare. I flinched. The sight of even one homeless person discourages patrons from entering the museum, so during the daytime the police keep the sidewalks in front of the building clear. That was my initiative. The desk clerks at the station now recognize my voice when I call.

I encircled the beautiful man's waist with my arm and pulled him closer, but I could see that we were falling away from one another in all the ways that count. It did not help that he wanted to talk. The more he talked, the farther away he seemed.

He said, "When you see a movie like that, it's hard to think about bringing someone new into the world."

He looked at the ground, with his fretful, nervous eyes and wrinkled forehead. Oh, how I wished he would stop talking.

Then he said, "I try to live a compassionate life. Do you think I'm compassionate?"

I allowed myself to study him. In some ways, in his calm and gentle manners, the grace of his movements, he could be taken for kind.

Instead of saying this I spoke another truth, which was horribly dawning on me just then. I said, "I don't know you."

It was his turn to flinch.

A bloating pain filled my abdomen. Pain. A new development. I buckled slightly and pretended I was bending over to adjust the zipper on my boot. I started to shiver also, but this was probably from the cold wind, which had blown in suddenly.

While the beautiful man stood waiting for me, he was peering down an alley across the street.

"There are people in there," he said, jingling some change in his pocket. He jingled that change, staring down the alley, as though he were struggling to be the style of man he wanted to become.

I stood up and examined the back of his head under the streetlight. I noticed white streaks in his hair. The photo he had posted online showed dark brown hair and a younger face. That whole night, I had been seeing the young man from the photo, and not the man who stood before me, a salt and pepper man, an aging man. His beauty would have such a short lifespan. For the first time, I felt that quality of tenderness towards him that I've seen adults devote to their children in childhood and other fleeting things, things you cannot put into display cases. Things you must let go. Some new understanding was just beyond my grasp, but before I could throw my mind into the void, he spoke.

Turning towards the alley, he said, "I'll be a minute."

"Don't." I grabbed at his turquoise sleeve and held it.

"Hey, money comes and goes."

"But time just goes," I said to his back, as he walked away and his sleeve slipped from my fingers.

I stood by myself under a streetlight and watched him walk into the mouth of the alley. I waited.

The man who had been asleep on the museum steps sauntered past me, across the street and into the alley, but the beautiful man did not come out. I wrapped my arms around my belly and watched three more men go into the alley. Then I retreated to the doorway of a darkened store-front and whispered, "Shit."

"Shit oh shit," I whispered again as two more men went into the alley. Still, he did not come out. My whispering moved inside my head because I did not want anyone to hear me, but it was louder, much louder, "Shit Oh Shit Oh Shit!"

Then it became much louder indeed, "OH SHIT SHIT SHIT OH PAPA SHIT SHIT OH HELP SHIT OH PAPA OH FATHER HELP!"

After I had watched a group of men leave the alley, none of whom were the beautiful man, I tiptoed over to the opening, arms wrapping my stomach, and peered in. There was nobody there. Just a long narrow passage formed by two windowless, doorless brick walls, with a twenty-foot chain-link fence at one end.

When I saw the torn scrap of turquoise fabric on the ground by the fence, I entered the alley and plucked the scrap from the ground. It was suede.

As I stood alone holding that material, the cold hollow

in my abdomen seemed to inflate. It grew so large that I felt it outgrow my body and I became lost inside the empty space of it. I stood there in an emptiness that was all pain and coldness.

Two men walked past the mouth of the alley. They looked in but not at me. The wind picked up the tails of one man's scarf. It was turquoise. The other man, from the steps of the museum, now had his lower arms and hands wrapped in two short tubes of turquoise, like the sleeves of a jacket.

He said to his friend, "He was beautiful, man. He was the most beautiful thing I've ever seen."

Or I think that is what he said, so nonsensical are the dispossessed. I had shrunk back against the wall and turned away.

With my father, some days are better than others. This is not one of those days.

The bedridden patient who cannot change position should be moved every two hours. Otherwise, sores may develop on the skin because of pressure from the bed. Moving the patient is easier with two helpers, but not impossible to attempt by yourself.

What happened on the night I went out with the beautiful man? I've retold myself the story countless times, using all the simplest, most threadbare words I know, but I cannot make sense of it.

Consider the patient's comfort at all times. Place a pillow under the patient's head before starting the turn. To turn the patient onto his or her right side, take the left arm, bend it at the elbow and rest it on the stomach. Then bend the left leg at the knee and tuck a pillow between the two legs. Place one hand behind the patient's buttocks and the other underneath the shoulder. Roll the patient away from you, then place your hands under the patient's hip to pull the body back into the centre of the bed. The patient will now be in a fetal position.

When my time ended with other men, I would wake up in the morning and have to remind myself they were gone. I would say, "Oh yes, so-and-so is no longer in my life. We will not walk through the park this Sunday." Or, "I expect I shall miss so-and-so but I will try to busy myself with other things." With the beautiful man, though, as soon as I open my eyes in the morning, I know that something is gone. I feel empty. When I say empty, I mean just that. I do not mean lonely or despairing on a spiritual level. I do not mean that my body is a symbol of something else. My body is not art. My body is just a body, earthy and base, sour breathed and polluting.

When I say empty, I mean that the cold that hollowed out my abdomen in the movie theatre has never left. I walk around with a hole inside my belly.

What I mean is that I have not bled in four months.

I took a pregnancy test, with hope, three times. Negative, negative, negative. I should go to the doctor soon.

For some patients, help with toileting may cause embarrassment. Be matter-of-fact. Replace diapers as soon as they are wet or soiled. After a diaper is used, clean the patient's genital area using soap and water, working from front to back.

Through our basement window, the twilight sky looks like a garish fluorescent sign, advertising . . . something. Night is coming.

Night is here.

The space between the two was so small I did not have time to prepare.

I drop my washcloth into a bucket beside the bed and say to my father, "This is my funeral oration."

"Nobody's dead yet, girl," he murmurs, smiling slightly and patting my hand.

I stroke his dry cheek with my thumb.

"It's just an old art form," I say. "It's the art of letting go."

And I begin the story again.

Wife, Mistress

The wife must rely on the mistress not to want too much of the husband's time. The mistress must rely on the wife to stay married to the husband. Neither the mistress nor the wife wants all of him or all of his time, which is why they tolerate each other and tolerate the husband's childish needs.

When the husband is with the mistress, the wife enjoys reading a book or drinking some tea and organizing everything on her writing desk just so. She does not have to listen to the muffled roar of television voices coming up through the floorboards. She does not have to step around the husband's enormous shoes tumbled together by the doorway or the coffee table.

When the husband is with the wife, the mistress enjoys the thrill of preparations – shaving, painting white crescent moons on her toenails and bleaching her arm hair. It is important to her to look nice and to see a man thinking she looks nice. When the husband sits on her stained futon, he stares at her from under his thick, black curls in a way that tells her she's gorgeous.

The wife sends the husband off to the mistress when she wants to relax. The husband wields his amorous hands like slabs of raw mutton, and the wife weighs only 102 pounds and bruises easily. When the husband is home, his hands are always on her mind. Always something to be considered or vacuumed around. When he is with the mistress, the wife can have a few moments with just herself, remembering who she is and gathering herself together.

The mistress sends the husband home to his wife after her neck and lips and thighs sprout red rashes from his stubble. He always promises that he will shave but then doesn't, and they laugh as he grates his chin over her neck and chest. It is one of their games. Another game is the husband claiming she seduced him, when really it was he who pushed his groin against her in the park. It is always a relief when he leaves.

To the wife, the husband makes general comments about women, which are really complaints about the mistress and mostly complaints about her slatternly ways. He comes home on some nights with dust bunnies clinging to his pants. At first, the wife gloats with the knowledge that she is still preferred. The winner. She picks the dust from his pants and admires her shining baseboards.

To the mistress, the husband talks about the wife. At first, the mistress sympathizes and nods her head, demonstrating that she does not have any of the wife's unfortunate characteristics. Between the husband and wife there is one point of acrimony that the husband complains about often to the mistress. The wife collects Japanese rice bowls, which she arranges in wooden boxes or hutches or china cabinets in the living room and kitchen. The husband cannot open a kitchen cupboard without seeing at least one tiny, painted bowl, but when he once tried to spoon his oatmeal into the grey ceramic, she snatched the bowl away and grew fierce and silent. Nobody, not even the wife, may eat food from the bowls. They are decorative. As the husband explains this to the mistress and how it hurts him, she takes baggies of leaves and herbs from her cheap plywood cupboards and makes soup, then allows him to choose whatever bowl he likes from which to eat it.

One night in bed, the husband touches the wife in a way he never has before. As he moves his hand gently on her, she feels in this caress the hand of the mistress. The mistress must be a delicate creature, thinks the wife. Very much like me. She imagines the mistress — benign and approving — watching from the dark shadows of the corner. The wife's body unclenches and opens.

One night in bed, lying next to the snoring husband, the mistress begins to cry because she is poor and lives in a tiny room above someone's garage. Whenever she opens her kitchen drawers, sawdust falls down onto her cutlery. It is hard to keep house in such a shabby space. After this, she lets things slide. She stops dusting altogether and forgets that out in the rest of the world, at art galleries or movie houses or historical landmarks, beauty exists. Where is her drug plan? Where is her pension? Why should mistresses not form a union? At the very least, the husband should be giving her gifts. Non-taxable benefits. She needs a can opener and a new coffee pot.

The wife begins to imagine the mistress looking at her bowls, touching them and retouching them with dainty, appreciative fingers. She wonders which one the mistress would pick as a favourite. Whenever the husband goes out for the evening, the wife stares at him lumbering down the driveway, sweaty from the heat of the shower, and pities the mistress. Or she pities herself, she is not sure. She blushes to think that another woman knows this man intimately, knows what the wife puts up with.

The mistress is younger than the wife and has not had children, and the husband goes on and on about her tightness. At first, she is smug, but then she wonders whether the untightness of the woman who bore his three children and raised them into adulthood shouldn't count for something. Life requires a constant balancing and rebalancing, a trading off of one thing for another. How has the husband not learned this yet? Why does he think he can have everything? She begins to feel affronted on the wife's behalf. He is like a child who has more than he needs but remains dissatisfied with all. Meanwhile, she and the wife have less than they need and, until now, have been content.

Shopping at a discount store, the mistress passes a bin of books. Shoved into a far corner is a picture book with photographs of ceramic bowls and vases. The mistress flips through the photos of beautiful things and forgets that the strap of her sandal is held in place with a large safety pin.

She forgets that shelves of cheap plastic objects with orange mark-down stickers surround her. She stares into the deep indigo of a ceramic vase and feels herself transported. The wife would understand, the mistress thinks. In one quick movement, she slips the book into her canvas bag, then escapes from the store. At the post office, she slides the book into an envelope and addresses it to the wife in her sprawling backslant. The words appear to unravel across the paper.

The wife recognizes the handwriting. Months ago, she found an address written by the same hand on a piece of blue paper, crumpled in the car's glove compartment with a receipt for expensive wine. Now, she takes a twilight walk past the address, which belongs to an apartment over the garage of a rundown bungalow. Her gaze lingers on the rusty iron stairs leading to a door above the garage. She notes, with approval, the potted begonias on the top step. She stands on the bottom step for twenty minutes, moving one foot onto the next step and then lowering it back down. She peers wistfully up at the door. Eventually, she goes home to the husband and sets the blue piece of paper on his lap. She does not get angry, but asks many questions about the mistress in a gentle, curious voice. The husband answers her while leaning forward on a garden chair, his legs tensed. They sit on the back deck until two in the morning when the wife kisses the husband lightly on the cheek and goes to bed. She dreams of the futon and the dusty cupboards.

The wife and mistress fall more and more into

sympathy. Why should the wife put up with clumsy sexual demands, the mistress wonders, and advises the husband to spend more time dropping petals into the bathwater and less time falling into bed naked and poking his wife's sleeping back with an erection. And why should the mistress put up with the husband's needling about unwashed sheets, the wife thinks crossly, as she puts a dirty glass by the sink into the dishwasher for the nth time that day. The husband now complains quite openly about the mistress to the wife. The wife advises her husband to allow women the same latitude he allows himself and not get so impatient. While he sleeps on her futon, the mistress nags him to wake up and get home to the wife. When he forgets to shave before going out at night, the wife berates him.

The husband begins to wear a guarded, suspicious expression. He paces the basement and jumps at loud noises. His hands rake through his thick curls over and over again until they stand straight up from his head and bob like grasses in a windy field. He is losing control of the situation with the wife and mistress, he knows. This is all he knows; he is otherwise helpless and paces the basement until his wife bellows down to him to come eat dinner now or not at all.

One day, the wife packs up her boxes of rice bowls and checks into a hotel. She does not leave the husband a note. To the mistress, she writes two words on hotel stationary: *I'm sorry*.

There is only one thing for the mistress to do. She

gathers together her cosmetics, her clothes, her nail polish and her baggies of leaves and herbs, gives her landlord notice and heads to the hotel. When the wife answers her knock, the mistress sets down her purse, and they make soup using a teakettle the mistress borrows from the front desk and the heavy plastic container in which she stores her hair dryer. Neither speaks, but both feel they know many things about the other. The wife opens a wooden box and takes out her two favourite bowls: one, burgundy with white cherry blossoms, and the other, blue with green marsh grass. "Ah!" the mistress cries, and claps her delicate painted hands together. Although her fingers are slender, her wrists and forearms are plump and soft, and wreathed in gold bracelets. The wife again feels something opening inside herself. They pour soup into the bowls and raise them to their mouths, peeping at each other over the rims.

The husband circles the city wildly in his car, unmoored, alone.

The next morning, two women carry bowls into a hotel bathroom, letting them fall and crack against the tile floor. They break every bowl but two.

Serial Love

Number 29 is talking about serial killers.

Number 14 squints at him across the table. Her squint is a mean, suspicious wrinkle.

"Yes," she thinks.

"No," she thinks.

Unlike other men in the nightclub – men wearing loose knit sweaters or brightly coloured dress shirts – Number 29 wears a black dress shirt with silver pinstripes. His black pants have creases ironed down the legs. Underneath the closely shorn stubble of his hair, his head looks uneven, dented in the middle and protruding on the right side. "Bullheaded," she thinks, as he blunders on in speech. She writes *bullheaded* down on her scorecard in jagged cursive, to remind herself later that he frightens her.

Number 29 has said that he works as a criminologist. She has said that she works as an indexer.

He has said he is thirty-four. She has said she is thirty-six.

All this may be true.

They have eight minutes to decide.

Already, Number 14 has decided that working as a criminologist is not the only way a man might know the behaviour of killers and rapists.

She studies the man across from her. While he speaks, his hands chop at the tabletop in unison, as though he holds a box between them and is shaking it at her. His box of facts and knowledge.

He says, "Do you know what an area of awareness is?"

She shakes her head.

"It's where perpetrators commit most of their crimes and where they feel comfortable, often where they travel between work and home and social events."

"What you're saying is that people commit crimes in areas that mean something to them? Near the people closest to them?"

"It's not my *opinion*. It's just the way it is."

"Why?"

He eyes the doorway of the club.

"For one thing, it's easier to commit a crime if you know where the escape routes are."

Escape is important for both criminals and victims, she thinks. Sometimes it must be hard to tell them apart when they're fleeing the scene.

"For another thing . . . ," he continues and offers her a tentative smile, suddenly ducking his bulky head as though shy. Then he stops smiling and his hands fall onto the table. One flutters, with surprising delicacy, to his jacket pocket and retrieves a pair of wire-rimmed glasses. When he puts them on, she cannot see his eyes.

"For another thing, everyone needs some sense of security."

The club reminds Number 14 of a subway station. Its low round tables, bar stools and walls are polished stainless steel, as though designed to withstand crowds of people flowing through on their way to elsewhere, and all evening, a crowd of strange men has passed in front of her. No sooner does a man sit down at her table than a bell is rung and he is up and off. After a while, it seems as though these are not different men, but one man who keeps changing his clothes and manner. A man in disguise. It is hard not to be suspicious of such a man – a man who keeps altering, like the landscape of the city, which is always under construction and covered with scaffolding, always getting torn down and rebuilt. Just as she adjusts to one view of the city, the next thing she knows, everything has changed. The buildings have gone from small to large or large to small and the familiar people are gone and unfamiliar people are in their place.

Two men before the criminologist, she meets a man who looks like a country singer, with his cowboy boots and square, bearded jaw, and when she asks him if this is what he does, he shouts, "Why does everyone keep asking me that!" He reminds her of her second boyfriend, who always shouted at her with reproach, so she ticks *No* on her scorecard. One man before the criminologist, she meets a man who owns a distribution business, but he will not tell her what he distributes. His silver rings remind her of the rings her seventh boyfriend used to twist around his fingers while crying over her indifference to his feelings, so she ticks *No* on her scorecard.

No, no, no. It begins to feel like indexing, breaking each man down into parts, putting the parts into categories. When she was younger, the world was broad and unknown. Now, she knows that world so well she can divide it up into index cards, which prevents her from making the same mistakes twice. She can squint at people, narrowing her gaze to a distinctive, mean slit, and bring them into focus – see them precisely and assess their faults by comparing them with similar people from her past. When her fifth boyfriend, a soft-spoken and gentle cellist, suggested that this restriction of vision might cause her to miss seeing a person's unique qualities, she stopped answering his calls; it had sounded like something her father would say.

Number 29 holds a clear drink, a lime slice pinching the side of the glass. It looks like a gin and tonic.

She says, "That's what my ninth boyfriend used to drink. I thought he'd drunk them all. I thought there were none left in the world, he was so thirsty."

Number 29 laughs, barkingly, but by the time she thinks to laugh, he has stopped.

"Ah, my ex-girlfriend was also sarcastic," he smiles, but then looks away. "She was sarcastic even while she was leaving our apartment for the last time and getting into a car with another man. Even then she still thought she had some right to sarcasm."

He leans back in his chair and eyes her across the table.

The bell will ring soon. Their time is almost up.

"I'm a feminist," she says. She brandishes the word as though laying down something between them, a bundling board in a bed, for instance.

"Yes, so was my ex-girlfriend. I could be *friends* with a feminist," he says.

Already, they are building their escape hatches, so when it comes time to flee the scene – and it will come, she thinks, staring at his shirt – the getaway will be fast and easy.

But! His hands have begun to dance out a new choreography. Now as he speaks, instead of chopping at the air, he dabbles with his fingers across the table as though laying out his words in rows. This seems familiar. This seems like what she does with words while arranging an index. Lulled by his dainty dabbles, she finds the chopping motion less violent and more generous when it returns. As he holds out his box of air to her again, she feels he may be offering her some intangible gift.

She throws one of her legs over the other and shifts both out from under the table, swinging her foot beside him. Then she remembers she knows nothing about him and sweeps her legs back under the table. Above the table, only her high-necked sweater is visible. Under the table, her black skirt barely covers her thighs.

She is thinking about areas of awareness, the familiar spaces where criminals commit their crimes.

"What about with bodies?"

He looks confused, so she traces the space around her hand, saying, "This is my area of awareness. But when I move my hand beside yours into your area of awareness . . ." she lays her hand beside his on the tabletop, so her thumb is millimetres from his own, " . . .whose area is it? Who is the more likely perpetrator when two areas overlap?"

Deviancy is an odd thing to flirt about, but he is smiling.

"That's not criminal theory, the body as an area of awareness," he says. "That's a theory of something else you're working on." His smile widens, and this time her squint relaxes and she allows herself to grimace in amusement.

They lean closer together.

Yes. Yes. Yes.

The bell.

After Number 14 meets six more men, the bell rings for the last time and she tears the white sticker from her sweater. The sticker has a one and four written in pink marker, no name. She leaves it crumpled on the bar and drops her scorecard into the slot of a box wrapped in silver paper with red hearts. She has checked *Yes* beside only one number – his number.

As she walks past him on her way to the washroom, he touches her lower back, fanning his fingers across her spine. Her body is in love. It has fallen in love in three seconds. With a hand. Of course, it could be the hand of a serial killer, she thinks, staring into her eyes in the wash-room mirror.

She is in disguise tonight, wearing four breasts – two real and two padded discs, cupping the real as hands would, as his hands might. She shudders with desire and trepidation, and one disc slides towards her neck.

In her twenties, she never dated people unknown to her friends or family, but in her thirties, she rarely meets single men so has thrown herself at the kindness of strangers, who could, for all she knows, turn out to be serial killers. Wasn't she taught, as a child, to fear strangers? But now the newspapers seem to be filled with contradictory messages. *Neighbourhood women warned of predator*, on page A2, followed on page D6 by, *Looking for men? Go out alone, look approachable, talk to strangers!* She sneers at such romantic advice. She imagines she will one day read a headline announcing, *Dark alleyways! A great place to meet men who are . . . looking.*

Everything seems backward, now she is in her thirties, especially because within the last year she has been suffused by hormones. Side-swiped and drop-kicked. They have interrupted her ordered life. They have careened through her bloodstream and made a mess of her schedule. She has heard people call this the biological clock, which conjures up images of babies and nurseries and pink crocheted blankets, but babies are far from her thoughts. Babies require long-range planning – savings funds, joint living arrangements, pooling of financial resources – while she cannot even think past her immediate need for sex. How cross this makes her. She has books to index. She has a manuscript on her desk right now, a book on trout fishing, but even this seems sexual, all its references to flies and lures. She cannot afford to waste time staring blindly at the pages and imagining naked boys parading among reeds and bulrushes.

So here she is, surrounded by men looking for women. The male sex drive is just what she needs. As focused and directed as an erection pointing right at her, which in its predictable simplicity sometimes reminds her of a silly Victorian parlour game. Oh, the infallibility of the male erection. It is straightforward. It is rock solid. And it requires only one index card, no subcategories, no cross-references. She remembers a tipsy date with her first serious boyfriend, fifteen years ago, when they had spent some blissful moments at the bar in a restaurant, licking one another's faces and laughing.

Although . . . although . . . she thinks about the last man she dated, who was in his late thirties and who, when she got him alone in her apartment, did not seem driven by physiology at all but was as fussy and fretful as a baby at a strange home, looking wildly about for its mother. When she sashayed towards him with her face tilted up, he back-stepped, as though worried she would devour him, which was illogical and aggravating. .

The indexer likes to think that this man was an aberration. Otherwise, if there is a pattern developing, she will need to learn new tricks, and it is possible that she is too old for that. Too tired and set in her ways.

How can people in their thirties learn new tricks?

She shakes her head and fixes her breast.

She knows men. How much could they have changed?

She imagines Number 29's fingers on her breasts, dabbling out their rows. She tries to reason it out. Even if he is a serial killer, perhaps he will not hurt her if she is willing and does not resist. In fact, if she is willing, she might never need to learn that he is a serial killer. This is the bargain she strikes with her reason.

It has been a while since a man touched her back.

She could leave the washroom and go home. The event is over. In a few days, if he has checked *Yes* beside her number on his scorecard, she will be sent his email address and he will be sent hers. They will need to take responsibility for whatever happens next. When she arrived, she signed a waiver stating she understood attendees were not screened. She released the event's organizers from any responsibility for what followed the final ring of the bell. Suspicion lurked at the evening's outskirts like a peeping Tom.

"I am willing," she whispers through her teeth, squeezing the taps. "I am willing." Her molars grind together.

She retucks her fourth breast into her bra.

He is sitting at the back of the club on a low, modern sofa, a white rectangle with steel legs. He rubs his index finger against his thumb, staring off into space. The tip of his tongue darts in and out of the corner of his mouth to the rhythm of his rubbing. She decides not to see this. Instead, she sits down beside him.

"So how many women did you pick tonight? How many are you going to see again?"

"Maybe I won't have to see any others," he says.

He offers her his drink.

"About that ninth boyfriend of yours," he says as she takes the glass, "my grandfather was an alcoholic." She sips and tastes only mineral water with lime. He takes back the glass and looks into her eyes. "I don't drink."

"And I'm not always sarcastic," she murmurs.

Over the next two hours, he fills in the details of a life that is placid and unthreatening. He works for the police and his brother teaches at the private boys' school near her apartment. He meets his parents and brother at a pub every Sunday for lunch. He owns a home in the suburbs just outside the city. One of his friends is a fireman.

While he speaks, her body – with preening self-caresses and head tilts – is holding a covert discussion with his. Her body is welcoming his, rolling out its little red carpets while doorkeepers swing wide the doors. She is barely aware of what her body is up to until she notices that she and Number 29 are sandwiched together, her hand on his knee, his arm around her waist. A great strategizer, the body has dumped doses of oxytocin – the body's Rohypnol – into her bloodstream to counteract her adrenalin, to relax and stun her.

They leave the restaurant to find night shrouding the streets and alleys. As Number 29 steps onto the sidewalk, night falls over his head and shoulders like a black hood.

He turns to face her, where she stands in the doorway, and holds out his hand.

"Come on. I'll drive you home." With his other hand,

he scoops a key ring from his trenchcoat pocket and whirls it around one finger — more confidence than he has shown all night.

His keys. His car. His area of awareness.

In the parking garage, he mentions that hidden eyes are watching her.

"Security cameras," he says, scanning the concrete roof.

She trails behind him as he points at beige cones poking from the ceiling like tiny beehives. She always thought they were sprinklers. She squints up at them and feels them staring right back.

She thinks about getting into his car.

Yes.

No.

"This is a high-risk society," he says, still looking up. "Terrorism, bio-chemical warfare . . ."

"HIV, hepatitis, pregnancy, serial killers," she thinks.

"I have a camera for a brain. I remember everything about tonight."

"What do you mean?"

"Sitting at the table beside yours was Number 26, a lawyer in jeans and a green sweater. Beside her was Number 10, gold barrette and contact lenses. I saw the rings around her irises. Then Number 12, picked at one of her cuticles the whole time we talked. Black wool skirt, run in her nylons. Then Numbers 20 and 18 and 4. And on the other side of the bar, 8, 16, 2, 22, 30, 6, 28 and 24. I could tell you how each woman dressed and how she behaved and what

she said. Five women wore glasses and only two wore jeans.
Nine worked as teachers. And you, you were Number 14."

Number 14 stops walking.

"I think I'll take the subway home."

He stops as well and turns to face her. "Why? Are you
nervous about me seeing your place? Are you married?" He
pretends to joke but his voice cracks on the final word.

The problem with his questions is this: she cannot answer them. She cannot say, "I suspect you might be a serial
killer," for if he turns out not to be a serial killer, such a
statement is an insult, and if he turns out not to be a serial
killer, she might want to see him again.

He takes off his glasses and blinks down at her, as
though he is just as confused as she is. Then he reaches forward and lays a large hand on her arm.

She sees this image – his hand on her arm – as though
watching it from above her own body, from the vantage
point of a security camera. Being seen by this anonymous
eye seems to displace her from her own body and even,
perhaps, having a responsibility for that body. She will just
let her body do as it pleases and watch what unfolds.

She smirks in what she hopes is a seductive manner,
and asks Number 29, "Do you wear a uniform?"

"I don't follow."

"At your job, do you wear a uniform?"

He steps back from her and takes his hand off her arm.

"No. Sorry. Women always ask me that. I'm sure I
could rent one if you wanted."

He turns away from her and moves between two

parked cars, saying over his shoulder, "People used to focus on punishing criminals once a crime had been commit-
ted, but these days we try to prevent crimes before they
happen."

He opens the passenger door of a black hatchback and
looks at her expectantly.

"Of course, security is all a question of balance," he
says. "Balancing caution against necessary risk. There are no
guarantees."

There are no guarantees, but there are safeguards.

"Just a minute," she says and pulls her cellphone from
her jacket. "I need to check my messages."

While he fiddles with his own cellphone, she lowers
hers and snaps a photo of the back of his car.

Then she texts a coworker, someone who might ask
questions if Number 14 stopped showing up for work.

"I met someone!!!"

She attaches this message to the photo of his licence
plate and hits send.

"Don't let them take you to a second location," she remembers a newscaster saying about serial killers, as she slides
into his car. "That's where they kill you."

No.

Yes.

She pulls shut the door.

They drive away from the city centre, travelling north up a
highway and then a series of side streets. She does not drive

and is unfamiliar with this route to her apartment, but he knows the area. His brother lives nearby, he says.

The car has leather seats and a CD changer in the back. She has never heard, before now, of a CD changer. He widens his eyes with disbelief and pleasure at such naïveté. As a female folk singer wails through the car's speakers, he grins about all the things he knows.

"Have you ever seen the houses along Arbour Path?" he asks.

When she shakes her head, he announces, "I'll take you for a drive then."

He turns down more and more streets, away from the streetlights and into a residential area thick with trees. She sways with the car, relaxed and dizzy.

High walls of stone and tightly packed evergreens, as well as wrought-iron security gates with cameras and intercoms, surround the houses. A jeep with the words *Securo Guard* written on one side cruises past. The houses look like sets from a movie. Massive Greek columns glow in the dark. Spotlights shine on the arched stone entrances of Tudor manors. These homes are not like anything an architect would design for beauty, but like something the owners imagined would be a grand home when they were ten years old. Number 14 stares at a stucco Italian villa and realizes that it is not a house but merely a dream of a house.

Number 29 points out five-car garages. He talks about what sort of house he might like to live in. What sort of house he has now. How many children it would take to fill his house (one) and how many children before he would have to move (two). He lays it all out like a banking plan. His voice drones on, nasally, but she is not paying attention. She is watching his large hands grip the steering wheel.

The houses are now farther back from the road, separated by vast stretches of dark lawn. She can barely see his face.

Of course, he will never own a house like this. These houses belong to pop stars and the Russian mob.

Even now, he is frowning and pausing at a crossroad, turning his head from side to side. "I don't . . ." He wheels the car to the right.

It slows to a stop.

"Oops, dead end," he says. He turns to face her.

They are on a gravel road, surrounded by the black shapes of pines. His headlights cast the only light. She looks at the uneven outline of his ridged skull, at the dark shadow of his face, at where she thinks his mouth should be.

It's him or me, she thinks. Him or me. Him or me.

And I am willing.

She smothers him with her mouth.

She tongues the hollow beneath his Adam's apple.

She shoves her hand under his sweater and pinches his nipples.

She pushes back his head with both hands, to expose his neck, and bites.

Only when his hands begin to dig into her shoulders does she stop. He has made an x with his arms in front of his chest, palms facing outward, pushing her away.

She grabs at his groin, but he swats away her hand and says, "I thought you were shy."

His voice is querulous and accusing, his breathing uneven. "I watched you at the club. You barely moved your hands or body when you spoke. You took up as little space as possible. Very shy people do that . . ."

"You profiled me?"

" . . .or liars."

The adrenalin that rushed through her body a few minutes ago seems to have pooled in her stomach, leaving her legs and arms numb. She feels tired. No, exhausted. The heft of her disappointment and humiliation, surely, will capsize the car.

"I have no idea how we're going to get back," he says, and she turns towards the windshield. The yellow arm of a barrier gate extends across the road in front of them.

They are both lost. They are lost in this suburb of designer homes with its illusion of security. A dream of a dream she had when she was much younger. Now she is older and it is time to learn new tricks. Bring on the new tricks!

She remains still, making no sudden movements.

"I won't hurt you," she says to the man who works for the police, and he whispers, "Liar."

Retreat

We spend our days working with old books and passing them, awkwardly, from hand to hand.

These books come from libraries with guarded doorways. Only after we pull identification from our wallets may we enter, and once inside, we do not even whisper, just mouth words into one another's faces. If asked why, we would say it is because we do not want to disturb other readers but, really, what we are thinking is, *We do not want to disturb the books*. Many have not been read in over three hundred years. It is as though they are asleep. *Hush. Do not disturb the books*. Our rumpled cotton clothing, often beige or cream, seems chosen so as not to startle the books. We believe they can be harmed, harmed as people can be wounded. In their fragility, we have a durable belief. Sitting at wooden library tables, we prop them on acrylic book cradles so the spines do not break. We use pencils rather than pens to take notes. Even so, in spite of all our care, the pages crumble as we turn them. When we try to brush the pale crumbs aside, they turn to dust and disappear into the grain of the tabletops.

Sometimes, when we are allowed, we check books out of the libraries and carry them back to our office, a small, scholarly publisher of a series of new books about old books. Our books will be read by few, will sleep themselves on library shelves, their spines unbroken. Young scholars are no longer interested. They can find images of the old books online if, in fact, they want to. Sitting cross-legged on their beds with laptops in front of them, they can examine the books without a special library pass, without relying upon our selections or editorial prejudices. Our knowledge of their indifference makes us gentle with one another, especially when we need to exchange books.

When this happens, we stand silently in office door-ways until noticed, on rare occasions brushing our knuckles against a door with apology. We insist that books be surrendered only if they are no longer needed, and we are only too happy to give up our own books in anticipation of their being needed. We stutter and interrupt one another in our attempts at politeness, and we never speak about ourselves, our personal desires or our fears for the disintegrating books.

We touch dry pages under the dim library lamps and then back at the office, behind closed doors, rub lotion into our hands.

Veronica comes to work with us on the day a confused deer wanders onto the street beside our office tower and spends two hours careening daintily through the heavy morning traffic. We suspect it will be shot as part of the cull. Deer have been a problem this year, invading our streets from a wood on the southern outskirts of the city. The wood is beside a lake, and we do not normally think about the lake, or the wood, or the deer, but now with a deer outside our office, we have to. We imagine, fleetingly, academics like us in the wood, holding rifles and wearing gumboots.

Of course, the shooters in the wood are not academics, and remembering this makes us tremble as though hunted deer ourselves.

The new employee, Veronica, is shouting from her office, "Does anyone have that book? I need it!" When we appear in her doorway – bashful, smiling and drab – holding many editions for her to choose from, she says, "Ah!"

At first, we find her attractive, almost mesmerizing. She wears a bright orange tunic over a simple, yellow sheath dress, and her dyed blonde hair is closely cropped. With the red of her sunburnt skin next to the pale blue of her eyes, her face appears volatile, as though the vital, contrary elements of life – fire and water – are both trying to exist within it.

"Ah!" she exclaims again when we hand her the book she wants.

Something is not right about her though. Something is not right.

It is not that she never gives us books we need, only shouts out what she needs, and it is not that she darts into our offices without knocking. No, it is her self-conscious carrying of books – she makes a point of carrying too many books in front of us. She will heap them into her arms, up to her chin, so we must rush forward with our own arms outstretched to prevent them from sliding to the ground. And she seems to do this just when we are most intent on our work, writing another diplomatically worded email to a distinguished British archivist, for instance, puzzling out each polite phrase and request. She will walk past our offices, the books beginning their slide from her arms, and we will rush to grab them. Then she will let her eyes fill with tears at her failure and collapse on a chair, so we must console her with murmuring reassurance. We find we are always putting aside our own work when she is near, to help her carry books or console her. It is exhausting. We stop helping.

"Looks heavy," we offer instead.

"Why not carry one at a time," we suggest, models of goodwill, while we move away from the plummeting books.

Something is not right.

Our phones ring rarely because few people outside this office know what we do here with the books. They do not need to know. If we worked and lived in a small city or town and had a group of friends and acquaintances, and if we went into the same stores every day to do our shopping, the percentage of citizens who knew what we did would be larger. In this large city, however, the percentage of citizens who know what anyone else is doing with their lives is small. People can get up to all kinds of things, or even slip through the cracks, and it does not affect the other people in any way.

"I have not had sex for eight months," Veronica says while we sit in the staff lounge together, reading newspapers and eating lunch. "I am a vegetarian and my last boyfriend wasn't. Whenever we fucked, I imagined a shrivelled, dry sausage pushing in and out of me. That's why I left him." Here she gives an anxious, wheezing laugh as though hyperventilating and looks at us exactly as she does when she heaps her arms full of books – expectantly. When we are silent, her eyes fill with tears. There is a nervous quality about her.

"You are in luck today as a vegetarian," we say.

"Monday is the vegetarian special in the cafeteria," we say.

Then we return to our offices.

As her problems worsen, so do ours. Her bike is stolen after she forgets to lock it to the fence outside, which makes her late the following mornings because she must walk to work. She misses deadlines, causing us to miss deadlines. She begins to complain of debt and ask us for lunch money. She fractures her right arm while climbing a ladder in the rain, comes to work wearing a sling and carries even more books on her injured arm, wincing and sighing loudly. But worst of all, she begins to spend time weeping in the bathroom. She weeps near stalls in which we sit trapped, fearing that if we emerge, she will fall into our arms and weep without stopping. We suspect that the weeping intensifies when we are within earshot. Hers is a reckless life of perpetual inconsideration. Why should her mess of a life be our responsibility?

How much easier to help her, to take on her troubles, if she were less . . . troubled. If only she behaved demurely in the office, and then we stumbled across her weeping quietly in a dark spot under the stairs leading down to the cafeteria. If we found her, engaged in this quiet, selfless weeping, we would rush to ask what was wrong, recognizing its seriousness. She would shake her head and assure us that really, it was nothing, and we needn't worry, and then we would promise to treat her to a coffee in the cafeteria sometime in the future, and she would change the subject. Later, remembering her momentary delicacy, we might hold open a door for her.

But perhaps such discoveries would never happen because we would never intrude upon a dark spot under the stairs where someone was sequestered.

"There are systems in place," we say among ourselves.

"Human Resources," we say.

"The Centre for Mental Health," we say.

"How can we be expected . . .," we say.

And then she comes to work in a bathrobe.

We go as a team to Human Resources and tell them our troubles, but it is hard to explain exactly what the problem is. It is hard to explain about the self-conscious carrying of books or why Veronica's presence in our office seems to promise our own dissolution. We do mention the tears and financial problems, and say she seems to suffer from an escalating nervousness. A woman writes down Veronica's employee number and proposes that we take an office retreat to the lake by the wood. She will make the arrangements.

Retreat, retreat. We think about the word in an attempt to understand what will be demanded of us. They want us to be more collegial and friendly, to emerge from our offices and emerge from ourselves, but also to retreat, which means withdraw. How can we emerge through retreating?

Two weeks later, at noon, we arrive at the lake in two vans. In the middle of a lush lawn surrounded by maples stands a group of small cabins, in which we will spend the night; the lake stretches out behind them. We are not used to such quiet and empty space, space where one could wander alone.

We cluster together on the lawn as the vans drive away, blinking and staring at the lake. Veronica says, "I have a mind to go down to the water."

And we, we realize, are of the same mind, so we walk together or, rather, walk a bit behind and to the left of her. We believe that she knows we are behind her – when we stop to switch a suitcase from one hand to another or readjust a knapsack, she has a way of stopping, turning her head to the side and looking back at us out of the corner of her eye until we start moving again. It is as though we are following her, as though she is the leader of this expedition, a thought that should be our warning to turn around.

But the midday light is so radiant.

She walks onto the narrow strip of sand at the water's edge. We remain on the grass. Not one of us can swim, and the water makes us nervous.

Veronica slips off her sandals and unbuttons her dress. Underneath she wears a red swimsuit. She faces the distant shore and removes her sling and splint before taking off her dress completely. The skin of her damaged arm looks grey. This is when she tells us that she intends to swim across the lake.

"And I have not swum anything in two years," she says defiantly.

We watch her from the place where the sand meets the grass.

"It's been two years since she swam."

"So she says."

"She took that sling off."

"So she did."

She raises her hands above her head, bends her elbows and flexes her fingers, moving her right arm more slowly than her left. She does not turn her head to look at us. She has moved down the sand, closer to an old beached row-boat. The lake is deserted, as is the lawn behind us.

We look across the lake to a cottage on the far side, its windows four white specks of reflected sunlight.

"That's a pretty far distance."

"About a half-kilometre."

"It's a lake . . ."

" . . .but a small lake."

We regard the rowboat.

The seating planks are splintered and worn. A few inches of water shiver in the bow.

"Someone should go out after her."

"Someone should."

She sinks into a few deep squats and then strides into the water, diving beneath it. She surfaces and begins a surprisingly strong front crawl towards the opposite shore.

Our breaths release in startled exclamations.

"Ah," we say.

"Ah."

How fast and confident her crawl. How radiant the light.

"I just remembered the day of my wedding."

"No, my graduation."

"No, driving in the car with my father."

"No, when I adopted my daughter."

"I thought the future was a broad, bold glinting like the lake."

"I thought it lay ahead like that cottage on the other side."

"It makes my breath catch."

"I can see it all again."

"I can taste it."

"A future filled with people."

"So many people."

"Who would come and go from each other's homes."

"Easily."

"Like water."

"Like air."

"No permission to enter would be needed."

"And I would not need to grant it."

"I imagined rooms overflowing with food."

"No, musical instruments."

"No, expensive clothing."

"No, trophies."

"I imagined gifts."

"Passing like water."

"From hand to hand."

"What a fine adventure to travel across the lake."

"My hopes are with her."

"Mine have already flown to the cottage on the other side."

We have each been with our own thoughts and memories, and each of us starts separately for the boat, although we cannot possibly all fit inside.

That is when we notice the dead deer. It lies between us and the boat, just behind a log, which is why we did not see it before. The log is black with moisture and rot. Water pools in the sand around it. The deer lies on its side, neck bent awkwardly, head tucked underneath, as though it had fallen head first, the body coming down after, on top. The gunshot wound is not a hole but a red stain on the lower right side of the belly. We have heard books called dead, but now we understand they are not – they are merely dry. They were never alive to be dead. The deer, surrounded by pools of lake water, with the blood-soaked hair and shining open eye, was a living thing that is now dead. Its living was never more obvious now that it is dead and still.

In the wood behind us, we hear a shot and then another. The second is closer.

Veronica is far out in the lake, kicking up water. Perhaps she swims more slowly? It is hard to say from this distance.

We stop at the log.

"She is almost halfway," we say.

Our voices ring out, but falsely.

"Look how strong she is."

"We, perhaps, were deceived in thinking her weak."

"Perhaps."

We turn away and walk to our cabins. That afternoon, we play volleyball and games where we fall backward into one another's arms with closed eyes. She does not join us. That night, while we lie in single beds beside the dark wood, imaginary gunshots fill our dreams, which die quickly when we awake to loud blasts in the early morning.

I cannot say what the others feel after we return without her, after everything is done that must be done, everyone involved who needs to be involved, every question asked, every form filled out. I cannot say what the others feel. I myself am rougher with the books and, on one occasion, even tear a page accidentally. I often feel as though I am looking at the world through this violent tear, and I have never seen it more clearly.

Baby Mouth

The mother drags herself through life. She is sleepy and for-
getful. One morning, she slouches into the kitchen, where
the baby is sitting in its high chair while the father spoons
cereal into its mouth. He says to the baby, "Here's your
mother!" and the mother looks around the room. "Where?"
she wants to ask. "Where is baby's mother?" But the baby
is waving at her. Opening and closing its fingers around its
palm like petals on a flower. *Remember me?* And she does,
thank goodness. She does. Feeling a rush of love, she bends
over to kiss each waving finger.

Without warning, the father pushes his face near the
baby's and yells, "Boo! Gotcha!" The baby remains serene;
it is busy letting a Cheerio turn to paste on its lips.

"Tough crowd. We'll get it right some day," the father
mutters, retreating to the sink for a face cloth. His dark,
bristly moustache curves down at either end.

The mother appreciates his efforts. She feels past such

theatrics herself, gnawed with worry about what is wrong with the baby.

According to baby books, average, healthy babies begin to smile and laugh during their second month, yet it is day 347 and their baby is still wide-eyed and solemn. In the hospital, it had beamed up at the mother while it lay in her arms, letting out a terrific smell from its diaper. The nurses explained that the smile was a reflex of the mouth's muscles, a response to gas, and not that darling of child care lingo, the "social smile." How unconcerned the mother was then. She assumed she would soon bask in the chuckles of her baby, but the days passed without even a grin. There are no end of books that list the stages of normal baby development – the mother could build a fort with all her books and hide in it – but these books are far less helpful about what to do if your baby misses a stage. She and the father consult many pediatricians, who tell them nothing is physically wrong with the baby and to "wait and see."

"What is the problem?" the mother now asks, as she does every morning. "What are we doing, or not doing?"

"To do or not to do!" the father shouts, as Hamlet, throwing out his arms and waving the face cloth in the air.

"Stop," she pleads.

"I can't anymore. I'm on automatic . . . what's it? What's that automatic thing?"

Fatigue is robbing them of words. Fatigue and baby talk. With every day that passes, the mother feels they are sinking further into the baby's world, the world of animal grunts and squeaks. She lifts the baby from the high chair and, doglike, sniffs at the diaper.

"Pilot," the mother supplies. "Automatic pilot."

But the father is already running in a circle with his arms spread, making buzzing sounds, looking hopefully at the baby. A suitor with plane wings.

In her arms, the baby takes a bite of air and then spits it out. *Pfffft*.

What she and her husband have been reduced to! They used to be bookish and discerning. She thought of them as the neighbourhood intellectuals, the father working as a re-search scientist at the Environmental Studies Institute, the mother teaching English literature at the city college. Now, she reads only baby books. Irritation flares in her throat.

She extinguishes the feeling and stops nibbling the ba-by's fingers. She has heard other women call babies "deli-cious," but she is not such a woman. She does not want to eat her baby. She does not want to harm her baby in any way.

Only five days after the mother carried the baby trium-phantly home from the hospital, the baby had a bad day. The mother had entered pregnancy with a theory – that babies, like adults, deserved pleases and thank yous. Deserved to have their permission asked. "Do you want mommy to change your poopie-woopie diaper?" "May daddy please wipe the ucky spit-up? Yes you did an ucky spit-up, yes you did!" She would respect the baby's boundaries, the perim-eters of its small frame, and in return, it would respect hers. This was how she dealt with her husband. But during those first days home from the hospital, boundaries grew fuzzy. They were especially hard to remember when the baby latched itself onto her nipple. And on the fifth day, the baby cried and cried and cried, so the mother held it for hours, taking it into the bathroom with her, bouncing it while she attempted to fold laundry, squashing the baby's foot between the ironing board and her hip. By the end of the day, they were both exasperated with one another. The mother tried to diaper the baby and accidentally stuck an adhesive strip to its raw skin. When she unpeeled the strip, the baby looked her squarely in the eyes and belted out its rage. *Oh, her cruelty!* it seemed to wail.

The mother reached down and gripped the baby's arms by the elbows. Then she jerked her own arms. Once. Twice.

All sound stopped. The baby's eyes lost their anger and filled with worry and confusion. So did the mother's. She backed away from the changing table. The baby whimpered the way it did at night, when it awoke alone in the dark. The mother found the father, asked him to finish with the diaper and locked herself in the basement.

Sitting in the dark of the furnace room, she battled visions of bumps, crashes and tumbling chaos. An hour later, she walked up the stairs and baby proofed the baby proofing, placing a safety gate behind the safety gate, sticking silver electrician's tape over the protective caps on the electrical sockets. She insisted they have wall-to-wall carpeting installed over the perilous hardwood. The following week she crawled around the new carpet removing every book, every knick-knack, from the lower bookshelves. Later, she cleared off all the bookshelves. The house, with its stark surfaces, looked unlived-in, like a newly won, furnished dream house.

She told no one that she had shaken the baby. Not the father, not the doctors. And now when the baby is not smiling, its eyes often dull and cloudy, any desire to tell turns a guilty cheek and runs. What if those two small jerks have harmed the baby? Caused a swirl of grey in its brain to come loose or unravel? But the baby sails through the other stages of baby development, moving assuredly into consonant sounds, sprouting pointed teeth that shine out from its mouth like raw gems. What could be wrong with the baby's brain? See how it gazes at its blocky board books, turning each page with an absorbed expression, just like a little adult.

Brain damage is not the mother's only fear. She also worries violence will burst from her hands again, without warning. She often feels annoyed. She grows irritated when the baby scratches her face with its growing fingernails; perhaps she says, "No!" a little too sharply when the baby hits its plate with a juice bottle; and worst, worst of all, on some mornings at 5:30, when the baby is screaming to be picked up, to start its day, she wishes it were not there at all. She wants it to disappear. Shaking a baby is not allowable, she knows this – she reproaches herself with it every day – but what about these thoughts? What boundary line separates the allowable from the heinous? Until she knows, she will treat the baby like an untamed animal, approaching with caution, doing nothing to scare or startle. Sometimes, she can barely bring herself to touch its vulnerable skin. The books are silent on this subject. They offer no guidance on how mothers develop a perfect, maternal love, free from irritation and resentment. There are no charts. Where are the charts? Only the unsmiling face of her baby gives a sign that she is flunking as a mother.

The mother is pushing the stroller, in pursuit of an idea. This morning, while wedging the baby's foot into a rubber bootie, she remembered a scene from an E.M. Forster novel, in which a baby's arms and legs are suddenly "agitated by some overpowering joy." She was so attracted by the kicking, bronzy limbs of this fictitious baby. A baby in Italy, a land of sun and joyous pinks and purples. Who would not be delighted in such a land? Who could not learn how to laugh? She will find a sunny patch and roll the baby into it. Perhaps on College Street in Little Italy. Perhaps in a coffee house with stucco walls and terracotta floor tiles.

But sun is hard to find in January, and the stroller's rubber tires stick in the slush. She passes by a storefront with white rattles and soothers painted on the glass. She peers at a green piece of paper stuck to the door: *in utero aromatherapy, the magic of colic crystals, tickle therapy*. Through the window, she sees a small reception room with a dusty, wilted fern and three empty chairs. No sun. The mother is not a user of essential oils or a believer in mineral magic. This is not normally the kind of place she would look at twice, but don't good mothers do extraordinary things for their babies? The baby shrieks and stretches its arms towards the passing cars.

Inside, soft, whispery sounds float from hidden speakers. Falling water and birds. The baby twitters in response. While puddles form around the mother's boots on the stained carpeting, a man launches himself towards her from behind the desk. He wears jeans and a brightly patterned silk scarf wrapped around his head, not a turban, but a pirate's head covering. A dot of gold gleams on his left earlobe.

Ignoring the mother, he kneels next to the stroller. "And what may we do for you, little one?" He looks as though he is waiting for the baby to answer.

"I was wondering about the tickle therapy," the mother blurts out.

"Is the little one sick?" the man asks, still gazing at the baby. "Normally, we offer that treatment to babies who are ill or in some kind of funk. Postnatal trauma and the like." His voice is soft, but every word is precisely articulated, as though its edges have been sharpened with a razor.

"My baby won't laugh or smile and we're way past the deadline for that sort of thing. We're supposed to be concentrating on other stages – drinking from a cup, walking."

The man looks up at her. His eyes are luminescent grey. The colour of a winter sky. "People shouldn't get too hung up on those dates. They are merely suggestions of time, not time itself. Every baby develops differently." He stands. "You develop with your baby."

She glances around the office, attempting to root herself

back in the world of the familiar. Framed certificates hang behind the reception desk. Printed words! Reading! But they are hung only close enough for her to see the gold and silver seals, not the writing. On one, she can make out the words, "Ten years of proven experience," written in large, loopy letters.

"You're here because you're a compassionate mother, a mother who wants what's best for her baby." The man brings his face close to hers.

She envisions, as she so often does, the grey matter of the baby's brain. A little piece flaps on one side, black from lack of oxygen, dead. The possibility of what can happen if you are not a good mother. If you do not want what's best for your baby.

"In the Middle Ages, lengthy tickling was used as a torture," she says in her teacher voice. "It won't be lengthy, will it?"

The man looks scornful. "We don't want to torture anyone." His eyes squint and regard her with suspicion, she thinks. He steps back. "You must open yourself to the experience. If you can't do that, it's pointless to try."

But it is she who should be suspicious! Ticklers are no different from practical jokers or people who pretend to offer something in an outstretched hand but then yank it back. She is *not* a tickler. When the father pokes at the baby's stomach, she always lowers her eyes. During their courtship, he once tried to tickle her and she curled into a tight ball and cried. It was such an invasion of space. Such an act of aggression. Surely those hysterical splutters and wheezes were not laughter, but nerves. Fear. A response to external threat. This is why people cannot tickle themselves. As a mother, isn't it her job to keep the baby safe from external threat?

"I'll think about it," the mother says and draws her lips together.

As she leaves the pirate's office, two elderly women come down the sidewalk towards her, picking their way through the slush. She wants to push the stroller back inside, but the women have already formed their faces into two pinched-up walnuts, crinkled and smiling. They have seen the baby.

"Hello, hello there," says one of the women, leaning down and peering into the stroller. The tassels on her pink toque wave. "How old?"

As always, the mother wants to lie. Claim that the baby is a younger, pre-smiling age. But it is too old for this game now, its large kicking limbs obviously those of an older child.

"Five weeks," she stammers, meaning to say fifty. She stutters, she corrects herself. The baby warbles and flaps its own tongue in imitation. When did she become so stumble-tongued around other adults? Maybe she always has been, but only since the baby has she realized it. Like a debutante ball, a sweet sixteen, the baby has catapulted her into society, drawing crowds wherever she goes.

The other woman — blue earmuffs — beams broadly. A plushy octopus hangs from the bar of the stroller, and she dances it in front of the baby's face. The baby's eyes remain dim. The women's smiles falter and fade.

Quickly, the mother says, "It's been a long day."

As if playing along with her lie, the baby begins to rub and muss the hair sticking out from its hood. Normally, it does this at the end of the day when tiredness descends like a warm blanket over its head. The mother wants to fix the hood, but she is always fearful of people seeing her hands. Worried they will spot the telltale mole or mark that identifies her as a wicked mother. Of course, her hands are hidden in gloves today, but they are not the only sign. There is also the soft, unsmiling smudge of the baby's mouth.

The women straighten up. "I'm sure," one says kindly, looking off down the street.

As the two women walk away, heads tipped together, the mother lifts her hands from where they have begun to cramp on the bar of the stroller. Inside her gloves, her fingers are trembling. Her reflection stares at her from the therapist's window, as grim and slackjawed as the baby's. Two moony-faced sulks in the glass.

"Eighty-five dollars?!" the father is saying. He stands in the middle of the living room, arms wrapped around his body.

"For the introductory assessment," the mother explains from the couch. "After that it is only fifty dollars a session."

The baby is patting the mother's mocassin and singing in a tuneless, baby falsetto. *Ahhhh, la la, ah, lalaaa.*

"But we can tickle the baby at home."

The mother has been waiting for this opportunity.

"They have special aids. They have ten years of proven experience."

Her husband scoops the baby off the floor and sits on the couch next to her. The baby spreads wide its tiny arms and flops onto his chest. Baby embrace. Its little mutters and coos soothe the mother and she drifts into a half-sleep.

When she met the father, she was wading through a Ph.D. in the Victorian novel. She spent her time at the library in a study carrel, a comforting womb lined with books. The father was studying molecular dynamics. He examined the integrity of molecules, what kept them together, what made them break apart. He looked upon their disintegrations as a tragedy, which is perhaps why he did not ask the mother to change her routine in any way. He did not presume. He just worked his way into her schedule. They already took their coffee breaks in the library basement at the same time, so why not sit together? They lived in the same graduate residence and walked to campus every morning, so why not walk together? It seemed so convenient. On Friday nights, it at least got her out of the library, where she would work for days on end, engrossed and unwashed, sometimes surprised by the rank smell that drifted from under her arms when she raised them. Other than taking more showers, she did not have to alter a thing. She and the father were radically content.

Now, suddenly, they have been thrust into life. There is life all around them. Suddenly, they have an unsmiling baby and a Cuisinart for puréeing carrots and avocado. Their time is no longer their own. Like a tragic molecule, the mother is breaking apart.

She opens her eyes to see the father looking at her sadly. "Hey, where are you? Where did you go?" he asks.

Her hands stroke the baby's wispy curls.

"Eighty-five dollars." He shakes his head, as if wondering how they ever got here. "All right. If that's what you want to do."

During the introductory assessment, the baby only swats at the pirate's probing fingers. When he strokes the soles of the baby's bare feet, it bursts into tears. The pirate recommends the intense treatment plan, which involves a prop – a long, blue wooden stick (from its length and broad rectangular side, the mother is sure it is a yard stick that has been painted blue. "Eighty-five dollars?" the father mutters, his face like a frozen lake). The pirate tells them that some babies need to get used to the idea of being tickled. They are more comfortable with a mediator, such as the stick, than direct contact. The mother knows she is more comfortable with a mediator.

But she still does not want to tickle baby, sitting so contentedly in its baby Trekker, playing with its fingers. Unfortunately, she will have to. By now, the father is perched on one of the chairs, refusing to join in the conversation. His suspicions are being confirmed by the minute, and he objects to being taken in. Like a great, shaggy bird, he glares down at the mother as she crouches on the floor.

The pirate explains he will tickle the baby first to

demonstrate. He presses the tip of the stick into the baby's green jumpsuit, right beneath an embroidered bear. The baby pokes the stick with one finger. The pirate draws the stick back and sets to repeated incursions on the baby's stomach. The mother can tell the baby is getting panicky. Its hands push at the stick. It swivels its head and gives her a wide-eyed, plaintive look.

She grabs the stick from the pirate's hands. "Now me," she says by way of explanation.

The baby thinks it has been saved. Saved by the mother, as it should be. "I'm sorry," she whispers as she touches the tip of the stick lightly to the bear. The baby accepts the stick as though it is a gift. Squeezes the wood between its hands. "Take it back, take it back," the pirate directs her in a stage whisper. She does. "Again," the pirate urges. She aims underneath the hands this time. If only the baby would laugh or giggle, if only the mouth would flower into something other than an organ of eating and shrieking, this could end. The mother's voice is imploring, crooning, "Baby, my baby, why don't you give Mommy a laugh?" But the baby is stubborn and defiant. Its face is turning red and its little legs and arms are curling around the vulnerable stomach. A frustrated grunting comes from the back of its throat. *Give Mommy a laugh so we can all get out of here*, she thinks. *Give Mommy something*. Exasperation pinches her throat. Exasperation with the pirate, his moist and excited breath on her shoulder, exasperation with her husband, sullen and unhelpful, and exasperation with – God help her – the innocent baby, who has gotten them into this mess. She presses the stick forward and gives a more forceful jab to the baby's stomach.

Its eyes glaze over and a shriek rattles from its throat. The father sits up. They have not heard this shriek before. Coated with gravel. Rich with an unfamiliar texture. "You're getting it," the pirate says. Tears drip from the baby's eyes as it stares at the mother.

Now the howl separates into pieces, tiny pebbles, which come hiccuping from the baby's mouth one by one. Against the weight of fast-flowing tears, pudgy cheeks rise upwards, squeezing closed the baby's eyes, so the mother no longer has to see their betrayed expression. But the mouth, oh at long last the baby's mouth, is lifting up at either end while the middle of the upper lip dips coyly forward. And the baby's chest is shaking and jumping in what can only be, what surely is, laughter.

Everyone is smiling. The father, the pirate and, most of all, the mother. It is as if a sudden ray of sunlight has bleached her thoughts and left only the sweet sounds of the baby's name singing in her head – the gentle whisper of the first fricative, the round rolling vowels in the middle and the final stop, which purses the mother's lips into a kiss.

She swoops down on the baby and pulls it to her chest. Its laughter, as it careens through the air, suspended between the ground and her body, delights her heart.

"There, there," she murmurs. "We're both scared, my baby."

Martin Amis Is in My Bed

I picked him up at a bookstore yesterday when I should have been writing, but I had grown bored with the sweet and sunny habits of my writing mind. I was working on a story about a woman and her life. The story contained potted herbs, moments of meditation in a kitchen and a final psychological revelation that was not meant to be a surprise but, rather, a reaffirmation of some comforting tidbit of wisdom that I assumed the reader already possessed.

Yesterday morning, I had stalled before the computer. I had noticed, with distaste, how my writing mind was forever clutching at the familiar word and the hand-me-down phrase. I paced. I ran my hands through my hair and twirled it around my fingers. Then I left my apartment and wandered into the bookstore where Martin stood, oddly, between Lorrie Moore and Carol Shields. My mentors. My *sisters*.

Lorrie said to me, "Honey, I only do what I can. I do

the careful ironies of daydream. I do the marshy ideas upon which intimate life is built."

Carol said, "Not one of us is going to get what we want. We ask ourselves questions, endlessly, but not nearly sternly enough. We're too soft in our tissues."

I looked at Martin.

"I have a hard-on for you a yard long, sweetheart," he said.

Quickly, I lifted the fraying corner of my cardigan and folded it around him. Then I skulked to the sales counter and asked the clerk to wrap him in brown paper.

So now Martin is in my bed, where he stayed the whole night because I forgot to ask him to leave. At this very moment, he lies tangled in the sheets by my feet, nuzzling my toes in the morning sunlight.

I spend the week in bed with him, strung out on sexual tension and the sound of his voice. I spend limited time at my computer getting any real work done. In bed, cars "shark around corners," people are "drunk and crazed and ghosted" and they "scream for cabs in the yellow riot of Broadway." The whole of England, it seems, has been "scalded by tumult and mutiny," by "social crack-up." At least, that's what Martin tells me. Those are his words. He likes words of upheaval, I notice. Of riotous chaos.

So why wouldn't I rather be in bed?

I should be writing, but . . .

Martin is leading me through a sultry merengue around my bed, giving it a lot of hip action. I stumble over the unfamiliar steps. I look down the hallway and see one corner of my computer through the study door.

"Ah, you women," Martin whispers, "edgy as hell . . . nerves spiralling to the ends of your hair, each with your special details of shape and shadow, of torque and thrust."

Oh, Martin.

And off we step-drag.

Later that night – much, much later that night – I gaze at the reflected outline of my face on the computer screen. Each person's mind bears its own distinctive rhythms and tempos, its own habits and inclinations. Staring at my face, I realize that I favour words that are impressionistic and pictorial, that float along the surface of things like sea fronds in a current (and, in fact, this sea frond business is the simile that introduces the story I've been working on). Martin, on the other hand, likes words that dig at the hidden and finger the raw, and in contrast, aren't mine just a bit precious? My hands tremble over the keyboard.

Martin, fearless Martin, calls out to me from the bedroom.

"You hot bitch! What are you doing to me? Come here and dance like a wet dream."

Oh, Martin.

I turn off the computer.

Instead of writing, I throw a party to celebrate Martin. I check myself in the mirror an hour before the guests arrive. For a woman, being associated with a man like Martin and his filthy, lively mouth can invite hostility, rage or, worse, insinuation. I close the top button of my blouse and tug my hem below my knees, but during the party I notice that Martin forgot to zip up after using my washroom. With his fly gaping open like a mouth, he roams among the guests, who sit in folding chairs around the coffee table. He enchants them with his views on pornography, booze and the strafing hostilities between the sexes. His ears blush red with alcohol. The last time I talked about sex at a party my words were awkward and veered between the euphemistic and the Latinate. I could not strike the right tone to say what I needed to say. What was worse, I could barely make it down the hallway afterwards without somebody rubbing up against me. Martin, however, makes no apologies for himself, nor does he need to. He is a success.

In the kitchen, I arrange endive leaves on a glass platter that belonged to my mother. I spread cream cheese into their pale green hollows and dot each with a caper. I smile at my work. I say to Martin, "Maybe tomorrow we could talk about me, sweetmeat. We could talk about my writing, just for a change."

Leaning into my arms, he slurs, "How much violence is crackling through the cabled tunnels beneath the street and in the abstract airpaths of sky? Every line that links two lovers is flexed and snarled between a hundred more whose only terms are obscenity and threat."

I stagger under his weight, knocking against the counter and setting the platter wobbling. Up until three months ago, when my mother died, she kept this platter and other fragile dishware in a cabinet, which she locked with a small brass key. Now, on its final wobble, the platter tips off the counter and crashes to the ground, fracturing into nothingness.

Later that night, while I am sleeping on my back beside him, Martin hefts himself over me and angles himself into my mouth. I wake up suffocating.

Thrashing out from under the sheets, I turn on the bedside lamp and look back at the bed, where Martin rests demurely on the far pillow. I throw him across the room. Our first fight.

Martin shrinks. This is the natural state of things in any relationship. The impact of the lover's physical presence lessens, but he is not *lessened*, oh no. Especially not Martin. For soon he grows small enough to fit inside my head. He takes up residence there. Sets up a bedroom with track lighting, black walls and a lush, white carpet. Sleeps in a bed under a bedspread with racing car checks. So although he no longer lays his long body over mine, crushing my lungs, he is now an inescapable, psychological fact. The *fact* of Martin looms much larger than the man who lay in my bed, who restricted himself to the physical world. The fact of Martin follows me everywhere – to the grocery store where I buy cereal (mockery from Martin about the dailiness of my life), to the hairdresser's where I talk about television (hooting derision) or politics (patronizing sighs). He becomes especially annoyed when I'm polishing my Paderno pots. I own a little grey cloth and Paderno pot polish, and whenever the pots get dull or a bit tarnished, I take out the little grey cloth and shine them up. I can shine those pots for a good hour, smiling into the reflection of my face and singing pop songs. When I do this, Martin will not even speak to me and instead starts up with a scornful humming like a lost television signal. He thinks I'm most facile, most fatuous, when I'm on pot duty.

I put up with his scorn because he has a point.

One day, I sit down at my computer and decide that my heroine will experience a precocious imagining in her kitchen – she will imagine that her heart murmur might make a sound like the "gentle cooing of mourning doves." Right before I type these words, from somewhere near my inner ear, Martin squeaks in a piercing falsetto, very unlike his real voice, "*a gentle cooing of mourning doves.*" A cruel falsetto. A mocking falsetto. An imitation of a woman's voice. Not my voice, but how a man might imitate a woman's voice if he were dressed in drag for a party.

I am so wounded, I cannot even move my fingers to type the sentence.

It is not that I don't appreciate the difficulties of his position, living in my head as he does, being at the mercy of my caprices and moods. He has told me that once a woman shrinks a man down and gets him inside her head, she can do whatever she likes with him in there. She can make him say things he would never say, engage him in heated debates about things he is mostly uninterested in. Oh, it is quite a playground women keep in their heads, according to Martin. An extensive, elaborate playground over which they romp, dragging their shrunken men behind them.

Thus, I resolve to forgive Martin his rude falsetto. Perhaps he is just getting bored, hanging about in my head all day. Perhaps he would like to share some soulful, earnest conversation.

I shut off my computer and ask him how he would like to die. I explain I would like to pinwheel backward into a snowbank, falling and falling until I hit the snow and sink in. Then the lapse into a big, embracing sleep.

Of course, I do not mention the frostbite, the frozen needles of pain, the clamorous shutdown of a system geared to fight for life.

Martin says he would like to sit on a bomb.

As he says this, he scratches his balls with a joyful vigour, as though pulling the words from between his legs.

"Just like a man," I warble in a high tremolo, as though I am now imitating Martin, imitating me. As though I am imitating my mother, surprised by the postman while bending over a calla lily in the garden.

"Just like a man," I say. "Leaving a mess for someone else to clean up."

An exasperated sigh chuffs up from the back of Martin's throat.

He retreats into the rank, fertile world of his own mind, scratching himself, invoking inspiration. And with me he won't share a drop.

"Just like a man," my mother used to say with disdain, as though nothing further need be added on that topic. My mother never spoke to her daughters of desire, or lust, or hate, or of my father's violent rages before he left her with three young children. When the evening news reported on physical assault, sexual attack or the murder of a woman by a man, my mother turned off the television as though keeping her three daughters safe was that simple, as simple as locking the china cabinet. "Just like a man," she might say as she turned from the television, before pinching her lips together. The phrase seemed a contradiction – reducing men to benign insignificance while also inflating them to the monstrous, beyond the pale of acceptable discussion. They were cartoon monsters who somehow, still, managed to perpetrate acts of unspeakable degradation and barbarity. To speak of these acts, to acknowledge them, my mother's closed mouth implied, would be an invitation.

Every time I sit down to write, Martin starts in. When I am searching out a way to describe a particular movement of the heart, a certain emotional lilt and sway, I hear his shrieking falsetto inside my head. Whenever he takes exception to my word choice – almost always – all he needs to do is repeat my words back to me in that mincing voice to show me how trivial, how foolish, how cloying, how trite, he finds them.

If only I could escape myself.

I type nothing new and Martin takes up scratching his balls as a habit. For much of the day, he sprawls across his checked bedspread, scratching, rubbing, fondling, jiggling, readjusting and patting.

I become quite fixated on those balls. Oh yes, the idea

of those balls is quite an *idée fixe* for me. Of course raw words ooze from him, I think, while watching him lean, heavy with alcohol, into his pillows. Such words are his birthright.

I slough off my old friends. Carol and Lorrie. Edith and Jane. I shove my friends into the study closet with my suitcase and photograph albums and slide shut the mirrored door. I've cleared a big space in my life and filled it with Martin alone. My old friends natter away in the study closet, but Martin's voice is the only one I hear.

I want to try it on. I want to wear his voice. I invite it in.

I write a character like Martin into my story.

While the heroine stands in her kitchen, meditating in the fading light, there's Martin, scratching himself and holding a bottle of Scotch. "I have a hard-on for you a yard long," he says, but it does not work. He is flat on the page. Nothing at all like the man whose company I shared during that first blissful week in bed. He hulks in my heroine's kitchen, taking up space.

I make him thrust a hand up her skirt. I make him fling hot stew onto her cheek and twist her wrist backward. I make him drive his knee between her shoulder blades. And finally, finally, before slamming out the door, he burns red lines onto her naked breasts with a hair straightener. The violence is not convincing though. Even the heroine seems unmoved, picking herself up afterwards and raising one eyebrow, alone with her thoughts and the charcoal-sweet smell of singed, blistering flesh.

Apparently, I am the only one left shaken and revolted.

I stop writing. I stop trying to write. I close the study door with a bang.

I sink into a television coma, watching one home-decorating show after another and picking at my toenails. I do this for three weeks. Although Martin does not like me writing, he does not like me not writing either. It gives him less to be foul about.

Since the day of my crack-up, he has tossed on his bed in a steamy, restless sleep. I suspect he drinks, among other things, when I am not looking. His room is filling with clutter. Empty bottles of Scotch and pornographic magazines. And one, two, three tired-looking women — women! — hovering in the corners.

Obviously, we are at the point in our relationship where *things* are beginning to emerge. Flaws that could be ignored before, when I was high on the buoyancy of fresh love, are now evident. He is too predictable in his vices. He doesn't even seem like a real man anymore but only an imposter — an idea of a man rather than a man himself.

An idea of a man rather than a man himself.

I experience a cold presentiment.

I walk into my long-unused study, flick on the computer power button and search online for images of the author Martin Amis. He is angular and lean, his chin tipped slightly up in all pictures, distinguished . . . dainty. He looks totally unfamiliar.

The man in my head groans in his sleep, as though ensnared by a nightmare. He mumbles, takes a gasping breath and then slowly opens one eye.

"Who are you?" I ask the man in my head.

"Who are you?" he bleats.

"Who are you?" I shout.

"Who are you?" he shouts back.

I beat my fist against my forehead in frustration.

It is all becoming clear.

I have trapped myself again, sedated myself with my own bromide – another clutch of clichés.

I have confused author with character, and character with caricature.

Something new is needed.

"Fuck off," I say to my own incorrigible invention, to my bloated, tired and aged child. "Just fuck right off."

Inside my head, the racing car bedspread is gone, the white carpet is gone, the clutter is gone. Everything is gone, including Martin. His room sits empty.

I remember Martin as he was in the beginning, a unique and peculiar man, whom I could still touch and be touched by. I remember the days when all I wanted to do was to become Martin, to climb inside him and stare out at the world over his nose and speak with his mouth. My hands wander across his face one last time in my memory. Goodbye. Goodbye.

I remember my mother and the vigilant gate-keeping she performed year after year to protect us. I mourn the choice that she made to hold herself in such opposition to the evils of the world that she died a caricature herself.

I gaze into the computer screen and have trouble seeing my outline in the murky morning light. I will myself to disappear, leaving just the empty study and its weight of possibility.

An empty room.

Anyone could enter.

Anything could happen.

And then I vanish.

Tall Girls

Jasper Marvin works in life insurance. Life *assurance* he calls it, thus fending off the hand-wringing fatalism of the word *insurance*. Its feminine nerves and fidgets. Its promise that something will, most definitely, go wrong. *Assurance* promises protection from the worst, like a heavy paternal hand on the shoulder. It promises a life lived in unchanging comfort. *Assurance*, Jasper likes to mouth through his thick, brown beard, savouring the word with his tongue, gumming and suckling it with his cheeks and lips.

He does not normally lean to the fanciful or the hypothetical. The fictive. He is quite without imagination. For a while, when he was seventeen years old, he was in the habit of striding into bookstores and proclaiming, "I hate books." Then he would thrust forward his chin and march out. In his early twenties, he began reading books with titles like *Prothinking*, *Proacting* and *Making the Best You Better*, books with bulleted lists and pie charts. He was then old enough to make distinctions. He would go into the same bookstores and announce, "Fiction – what's the point?" and cruise, with purpose, over to the tables of business books.

Although he lacks imagination, he is not without sensuality. He loves the physical world, and why wouldn't he? It never disappoints. He strokes the leaves of potted plants, slaves over complicated sauces on his stove and finds an ecstasy like no other in the scent of the skin between a woman's collarbone and underarm. As a lover, he is fiercely competent, enjoying the transformations of the female body in bed. Its softenings and swellings.

Only lately has he noticed a change in the female form. One that disturbs him. The realization was forced upon him three days ago when he stepped off the subway. Suddenly, a collision. A feminine smell of laundry and hand soap. He readied himself to look down, apologize graciously, offer a sympathetic arm or word. Turning, his glance was level with her nostrils. She had barely registered his presence and breezed past him onto the subway like a wind above the mountains.

After that, he saw them everywhere. Tall girls. Girls pushing six foot three, heads sweeping the sky. They were stooping under door frames, crowding the buses, loping past red lights at the crosswalks. Robust and vigorous, these girls had ruddy cheeks and the uncomplicated gaze of Olympic athletes. Wherever they went, they carried knapsacks slung across their backs, with bottles of water sticking from the pouches. Jasper's mind filled with something unfamiliar – speculation. What might these knapsacks hold? He imagined sporting equipment, running shoes or electronic devices that strapped around the chest or ankle and measured heart rate, breathing, miles crossed. Unnoticed, these girls had been growing for years, with the knowledge of proper exercise, good nutrition, reaching their potential. And then, all at once, they were full-grown and everywhere.

Today, Jasper is peering from the fourth storey of his office tower onto the street below, looking for tall girls. How easy it would be for a tall girl to grow hunched and self-conscious, but these girls hold their bodies with un-selfconscious pride, completely free from an awareness of anyone looking at them. They are only aware, or so Jasper imagines, of how good they feel inside their own skin. Perhaps humankind has reached another point in history when it undergoes a growth spurt (he remembers photographs of tiny chairs and tables in English Tudor homes), and then all the furniture, the equipment of everyday life, is too small.

How to meet a new epoch? Not only will there be physical changes, but a mental shift. Just look at his own strange, unexpected thoughts. His burst of whimsy. He's read about this. *Paradigm shift*. He mouths the phrase, but quizzically, without confidence. His lips wobble, his jaw shivers. New thoughts will be struggled with and coaxed into being. Demands will be made. But of what sort? His narrow imagination cannot foresee the consequences.

For the first time, he realizes he possesses something that is too small.

Two months later, a tall girl with long, red hair moves into Jasper's three-storey walk-up. The unit above his. All morning he watches her from his window as she directs the movers in and out of the front entranceway. She brushes past him in the lobby when he is leaving to run some errands, giving him time to study her height. She has an extra inch on him, a looming fraction of a foot. And now, as he is returning home, here she comes up the front steps, embracing grocery bags in her long arms (he is sure she could carry anything in the immense cradle of those arms). Out of the bags rise glowing salmon fillets, the dense greenery of Swiss chard and a tub of frozen blueberries. She bears down on him, a loose-limbed giantess.

"Antioxidants," she announces, not so much *to* Jasper as near him. She gestures with the groceries and sweeps past, trailing the scent of herbs and fish.

"Yes," he murmurs, in awestruck wonder, "yes," as though this revelation is what he has waited for his whole life. "Antioxidants." He spins the unfamiliar word over his tongue and watches her turn the corner, without a backward glance. He leans against the wall, breathless and bone-shaken.

He is unable to call her back. He is unable to charge forward and accompany her up the stairs. At her doorway, there would have been loitering and pleasantries and a dinner invitation. He would have made her a cream sauce. But the air feels too heavy to move through or to shape with his mouth to form words, and the wall pushes oppressively against his back. For the first time in . . . well, he can't remember how long . . . the world is not cooperating with his plans.

And then right in front of his eyes, in the empty place that she has just left, the unexceptional hallway, the air appears to bevel and shudder. The real becomes hazy and the hallway divides into two hallways – the hallway in front of his eyes and another hallway, somewhere behind them. Somewhere in his mind. The second hallway is filled with viscous shapes and unclear sounds. He shakes his head and plunges a hand into one pocket, clutching at the reassuring weight of his keys.

"Have you noticed that the girls are getting taller?" Jasper asks, breathing heavily into his beard. Sweat drips into his eyes.

He is running on a treadmill beside other men from his office. Their hairy knees plunge up and down in unison. The ground floor of their office building holds a gym, to which they retreat after work in suited camaraderie. The presence of other men makes Jasper run harder than he would if he were alone. They challenge each other's limitations, not so they can run long distances outside, not so they can forge for miles across the land and chart a course into the horizon, but so they can run faster, farther, on the treadmills the next time. No matter. The horizon line has long been a memory. If Jasper was to set out towards it, he would run smack up against the side of a building.

On one side of him, a man is fiddling with the nozzle of

his water bottle. Without looking up, he says in answer to Jasper's question, "Chlorinated water."

Another man says, "Bovine hormones."

A plump woman hops off an exercise bike in front of them and joins the conversation. "Yes, it's the hormones in the milk. I read something." She scrutinizes the legs and hips of a woman on the bench press.

The man with the water bottle says, "I've noticed their breasts. Just twelve-year-old girls with breasts." He says this with such distaste that it sounds as if the girls have been sprouting cow udders.

"They're having sex too young."

"They're menstruating earlier."

"They know too much."

"They've lost their innocence."

Everyone's eyes dart suspiciously to the plate glass window, as though worried a herd of hormone-filled adolescent girls might come stampeding through the glass.

"I think we're getting away from the point here," Jasper remarks. "I just want to know why they're taller."

Suddenly, he sees the tall girl's hair. Not here in the room with him, but in his mind. Like the other day in the lobby of his apartment, the world has divided itself into two — what he can see in front of him and what he can see somewhere behind his eyes. But today, from the swirling shapes of that inner world, a clear picture emerges. The sunset streaks of red and orange that are the tall girl's hair. And be it the rhythmic motion of Jasper's legs or the damp smell of his sweat, the vision is richly erotic. His feet stumble on the treadmill, and he plants them on either side of the moving belt to regroup.

It occurs to him that he can shape this vision into anything he wants. That there is a new power here, in his own mind. A word crosses his lips. *Fantasy.* Is this it? He has never experienced an erotic fantasy. He is not like the women he knows, whose auto-erotic activities take minutes and minutes of premeditation. Who might even fall asleep before what surely is, even for women, the main event. His own auto-erotic life is based on brief impulses and reaction. No sooner agitated than relieved. There is no mental effort. No unfolding story. He has never had that skill, which is why he sometimes relies upon magazines or movies. The whole of his fantasy life would not make up a novella or even a limerick. A breast, a wet mouth, fingers under nylon, that is all and then it is over. But now . . . this image of red hair burning behind his eyes.

In the change room later, he sits on a bench, trying to gather pictures from his mind and fit them together, but he is unpractised. He manages just this – there is an empty doorway, and then the tall girl is in the doorway, wearing a long peach coat. It is some kind of shimmery plastic material. She stands in the doorway. He waits. Where will his fantasy go next? Where can it go? He can't fathom the possibilities. He can't get her through the door.

He leaves work eager to explore the potential of this new gift, this strange seeing. He has always equated fantasy with pornographic images, which he thinks of as dark and heavy, like moist soil between his fingers. But the moving shapes and shadows in his mind now are not heavy at all. They fill him with incredible buoyancy, as if his feet are leaving the ground, as if he is leaving the rest of the world behind.

This much is obvious – he needs help in shaping his own first erotic story. Try as he might, he cannot reign in the racing shadows in his mind. On his way home, he stops at a corner store and quickly grabs six of the glossiest X-rated magazines from a high shelf. As soon as he has them in hand, he feels comforted, solid again. He also feels very, very hard.

He decides to make a collage, of sorts. He takes his task seriously. Although he is not painting, he changes into an old shirt to enhance the feeling of dangerous artistry, of *anything could happen*. Sitting at the head of his dining room table, eight feet long and solid oak, he spreads the magazines around him, flipping pages with a critical eye and stroking his coarse beard. Wild artist. He growls deeply and admires his large and competent hands as they work the scissors.

A few snips and he has a pile of skin-slick pictures, a glistening heap of peaches and tawny browns. The pictures feature tall redheads with some expression in their eyes. An expression that suggests a continual motion around the frame of the photograph. Something happening after or before the picture was taken.

He arranges the clippings to form a storyline. Here is how it goes: woman in red garters lifts up her red skirt, woman in white skirt removes her top, woman suddenly without clothes lies back invitingly on a desk. Suddenly, she is holding a tea towel and lying on a carpet. Suddenly, she is standing on a rooftop patio overlooking a city.

It doesn't work.

The images refuse to turn into the tall girl or wind together in any meaningful way. Jasper had hoped that once he lay out the photos, he could become a passive viewer, an audience member of a movie he had set in motion, but more is obviously required. He is distracted by questions he cannot answer. Why would a woman stand on a roof, naked? She is apparently only admiring the view, arms leaning on a railing, but he himself is a private person and cannot imagine anyone stripping down on a rooftop. Surely the railing would dig into the bare flesh of her arms. He notices a scrap of paper in one corner of the photo, against an iron grill. Is this a clue? Perhaps, but he cannot interpret it. And how would she get, naked, from a room in the building where she was cavorting with a tea towel, up to the roof? If she got dressed again, and then undressed at the railing, the mood would fade. And he doesn't see any discarded clothes at her feet. How can he get around the presence of the physical world in his fantasy? Ignore its tedious yet pressing demands?

The inner eye that opened at the gym remains stubbornly closed.

His hands lie, limp and useless, on the tabletop. Failure.

With a sweep of his arm, Jasper sends his day's work fluttering into the wastebasket beside the table.

The tall girl comes home and he hears her moving above him. The thump and jangle of sandals hitting the floor, running water, the muffled clank of pots.

His head and balls ache. He goes for a long, purposeful walk. On this walk, he touches telephone poles, stop signs, mailboxes, concrete dividers, iron fence rails. He touches doorframes and garbage bins and plastic chairs outside of bars. Waiting at a stoplight, he leans forward and grasps the tail of a dog in front of him. He touches all these things to bring himself back. To reassure himself that he is still in control of the real.

Jasper begins sending things to the tall girl's apartment, from places that will keep his name and address a secret. He sends a silky nightgown and two crimson camisoles from a mail order catalogue. He browses the perfume counters at a department store and picks three of his fa-vourites – all with sweet baking smells. The department store will not agree to deliver the perfumes alone, so he also orders a new Durafoam mattress. He stretches out on it in the store, closes his eyes and imagines the tall girl lying exactly here. He realizes he is furnishing a bedroom, no, a boudoir. He smacks his credit card down on the counter with new confidence. He discovers online order-ing and orders wine-coloured satin throw pillows, as well as a heating blanket that vibrates. He wonders briefly if he's going too far. If he's becoming one of those men he reads about in the newspaper. But by now he's thinking in clichéd song titles – *Baby how can this be wrong if it feels so right?* He has the money and nobody, no wife, no kids, to spend it on.

And what is he buying? An image, an image of a bedroom that he knows intimately. Down to the corrugated foam and silk ticking of the mattress. He is finally getting somewhere. He is closing in on something. Three weeks into his buying spree, he crouches on the floor of his bedroom. A picture of his purchases, assembled in a room, floats clearly in his mind. He can see the tall girl on the bed! Radiant in crimson and silk. She flicks the white plastic dial on her blanket and the blanket begins to hum. She beckons with one finger . . .

And then, in one corner of the picture, a splotch of grey. Beside the bed on the floor lies a pair of thick grey socks that he bought last week from the Outdoorsman. *A miracle of science!* the package claimed. Cool in the summer, warm in the winter. Made to wick away moisture. He bought three pairs in different sizes and dropped them in front of the tall girl's door. He imagined she was a walker: the beach in the summer, snow-covered forest paths in winter. He imagined she might need socks just like this. But how do they fit into the sex he's been picturing? How can he make the socks fit? Perhaps he and the tall girl have just returned from a camping trip? A ski weekend? This conjures up a whole host of unfamiliar terrains and props that are not in the script. And anyway, perhaps they don't fit. Perhaps, perhaps, in the end, they are just socks. As unremarkable as the quotidian odds and ends of real life. His narrative, with its carefully spun threads, unravels like grey acrylic microfibre. Once more, she has eluded his imagination.

He wraps himself in a long cardigan and slouches from his apartment. Opening his mail in the lobby, he sees credits piled up on his credit card statement. She has returned his gifts. In the hallways, her expression remains placid and distant. The world is as it was.

The world is not as it was. At work the photocopier mauls his originals, the coffee machine spits up on his tie and the fax machine spews a list of meaningless letters and numbers. He arrives at his afternoon meeting rumpled and stunned. He sits down and glances to the left, at the delicate hand of a woman beside him, curled around a glass. Each finger tapers gently, past its whorl of dark pink knuckle. A sweet ache rises to his throat, where he always feels desire first, as though he is breathing in hot tar. Around the hand the meeting room folds and collapses.

The hand passes him a spiral-bound booklet and a highlighter. Then a memo. At the front of the room, someone is doing something artful with a spreadsheet. He wonders, in one of the imaginative bursts of insight that are becoming more frequent, if all this, these buildings, these meetings with their delicate social balances and mincing diplomacy, these mountains of paperwork and emails, are only a substitution. A diversion. To prevent people from spending all their time leaping into bed together. From fucking and fucking and fucking and fucking.

He needs to touch the tall girl. To see her with his eyes as clearly, as distinctly, as he can this hand.

When he comes home late, after nine o'clock, he slinks around the back of his building and gently scales the fire escape. The daylight has gone. On the third storey, he stops and tries to peer through a frosted window. There is only a small line of clear glass around its edge. The room within is dark, so he huddles in his place for a few minutes, between the recycling bin and a blue plastic garbage can.

A square of light opens in the darkness. The tall girl is entering her apartment, carrying keys and grocery bags. She is at the far end of a hallway. She walks towards the window, clicking on lights, and Jasper sees that the room he is looking into is the kitchen. She covers the counter in bags. She scratches her elbow and takes a moment to examine its roughened, grey skin. Jasper's breath is a flurry of moth wings in his throat. She is close, very close, unloading household items. Tomatoes, shampoo, a box of cereal. Freckles cover the firm swell of her upper arms, and the outside corner of her left eye narrows into a tiny scar.

He places both hands under the lip of the window.

Longing for a violent physical connection riots inside him. Not in his mind, but his muscles. He is in his body more at this moment than he has ever been. He *is* his body.

His fingers brace themselves on the window, his arms tense.

Suddenly, with a swift motion of her long arms, the tall girl throws open the window, sending it rolling and

groaning upwards on its rope. The force of that one gesture causes Jasper to fall backward onto the steps of the
fire escape.

Thrusting her head and upper body out the window,
she takes a deep, gulping breath of night air. In her right
hand she holds a ball of plastic bags, which she drops into
the recycling bin underneath the window. "Apologies," she
says, as she notices him quaking on her fire escape. One
long arm shoots from the window (later, he will wonder how this was even possible, this tremendous distance
she reached), grasps his wrist and yanks him upright.
Perfunctorily. As though she is tidying up. He flies upwards
like a blade of grass plucked by a giant.

"Nice night," she says in parting, as though he has
merely been taking in the air. Then she ducks back into her
kitchen, leaving the window open. Her hand flicks out and
brushes a wandering ant off the sill. The banging of cupboard doors resumes.

She withdraws a large beet, brown, hairy and rough,
from a bag and places it on the window ledge, in front of
his eyes. She disappears from his sight. Without her in front
of him, the energy streams from his body like a downhill
river, coursing from his feet. He is shaking. He slinks back
down the fire escape.

That night, he dreams of root vegetables. Also root rot
and dirt. He dreams of inescapable gravity, pulling him to
the ground. He dreams of the tall girl in a room with him at
last. At last. But the camera of his dreaming mind will not
stay focused on her. It keeps wandering to the wallpaper,

which is painted with radishes and turnips. Squashes tumble awkwardly from his pockets. He reaches out to touch a freckled arm but can't. She is wearing a protective amulet in the shape of a carrot.

When he wakes up he stares at the ceiling, the boards that separate him from her. There will always be this distance to bridge, this height to cross.

He has no power over her life.

For the first time in his practical, assertive existence, he is flooded with despair. He gives up. Surrenders. A passive lethargy invades his limbs. He allows the tide of it to carry him out, far out, to sea where his body floats like a discarded object on the surface.

His mind goes under.

It dives away from his body, jackknifing into the murky deep. And there – there! – a portal opens wide, revealing a miracle of vibrant colors and sounds. Images hidden until now.

They are ripe and everything he has waited for.

Hysteria

Alisa picks up the phone to hear the doctor shouting at her – "The lab found blood! I think we're onto something!"

Not such a remarkable discovery, Alisa thinks. The dark orange clot, like a sea creature with waving tendrils for arms, was easy enough to spot in her urine sample although she understands the doctor's excitement. For weeks, her complaints were the only evidence of the pain in her pelvis, but now the doctor has proof of an illness. Without proof, his normally assured voice had begun to stammer during her appointments. But blood! That's something he can work with.

The doctor continues, "Bring yourself in for more tests," as though her body is a misbehaving dog that she hauls around on a leash.

It is then that her head splits from her neck and hits the bedspread with a muffled *thwump*.

The phone drops to the floor.

Neither head nor body bears a wound – nothing open

or raw or painful. On the thin stump of neck left above the shoulders, the head sees a covering of soft skin, like that on the underside of the forearm. And when the body gropes with tentative fingers beneath the chin, it feels the same smooth skin. Although head and body continue to perform some things as a team – the lungs inflate with oxygen when the head inhales, for example – they are otherwise separate. Really, thinks the head, blinking up at the body from the patchwork bedspread, the separation feels quite natural. As though head and body have been divided for years.

When Finn comes home from his office, clutching a bottle of red wine in his spidery fingers, he finds the body stretched out on the bed wearing a frayed, green terry cloth robe while the head glares at it from a wicker chair in the corner. Finn says nothing. He is a gynecologist and spends each day with his hands up other women; he is used to thinking about women's bodies in isolation, separate from their heads.

"So now the body is *bleeding*," the head announces with contempt.

The body shrugs and sprawls smugly across the bed, like royalty in a palanquin. Since the doctor's call, it has carried itself with the self-indulgence of the sick, moving with luxurious, expansive motions and taking up space. Against the head's wishes, it swanned around the house all day in the ugly robe, neither showering nor getting dressed.

Finn walks to the bedroom window and stares at the pine branches pressing against it. Their bungalow is in a town of bungalows on top of an escarpment, a high ridge of rock. When he turns from the window to the bed, he sees the body, like the escarpment, stretched out in stony solitude, isolated from all around it.

Looking only at the head, he says, "It's Friday." He wiggles the wine bottle. "But I guess . . . should we? No . . . or perhaps . . .?"

"No, Finn," explains the head firmly. "Not this Friday."

So Finn carries the head out to the living room where they watch television. The body lies in the darkening bedroom alone.

The body has become an embarrassing relative, and the head wants nothing more to do with its failings. When they are in the same room, the head sneers and gazes off a sufficiently superior distance into space. True, pain from the pelvis continues to thrum through peripheral nerve fibres and up the spinal cord to the brain, jumping the space between body and head as though travelling across a large nerve synapse, but at least the pain feels muted. And perhaps the head will no longer need to accompany the body to doctor's appointments, where it could never reconcile its modesty with the indignities of the doctor's examinations and was forced to imagine itself floating away from the body and hovering somewhere just beneath the ceiling. Perhaps from now on the head will be allowed to stay at home. After all, it is far from the pelvis.

The doctor makes this clear at the next appointment when the pouting head, cradled in the body's arms, asks, "Do *I* really need to be here?"

"Why would we need you?" The doctor looks cornered and defensive. His stammer returns. "D-d-did I imply that? When did I imply that?"

The head flushes with relief. When it was still attached to the body, it spent many evenings fretting and chewing on its cheeks, worried that because the doctor could not find a problem with the body, he would blame the head. He would accuse it of hysteria. (Here, the head always imagined a parade of repressed Victorian women with paralyzed limbs, stuttering tongues and strange coughs, conditions all rooted in unexpressed emotional disorders.) Hysteria. Hysteria. The head grew hysterical even considering the word, but obviously the doctor was no fool. He did not want a horde of angry, modern-day women storming through his office waving placards, upturning chairs and burning effigies of Freud. Staunchly, he kept ordering more tests, signing his name with a flourish to pink pieces of paper, his jowls quaking like a bulldog's, until he got the results he wanted.

The doctor leans forward reassuringly and looks at the body. "This isn't in your head. It's a *real* problem. A real physical problem. Prostitutes, for example, suffer chronic illnesses of the urinary tract."

He smiles with benevolence.

"We don't tell women it's in their heads anymore." A bullish, amused snort explodes from his nose. "That's archaic. And besides, you are bleeding."

This is the body's problem, and the body's alone.

The doctor says that the specialists will now take over and perform some tests. Conversation won't be necessary.

"In future, you might as well just stay home," the doctor says to the head, sending it a quick sideways glance. "The urologists and radiologists don't work with h-h-heads."

Finn paces the bedroom. He is talking to the head, which rests in its wicker chair beside the bed. The body sits with its back against the headboard, calmly filing its nails. It spent the day spoiling itself, lying in the bath for three hours and then rubbing an expensive lotion onto the corns on its feet.

"But it's Friday," Finn explains to the head. "And I like to think we have a healthy bedroom life. So let's just give it a try." He fidgets with his silk tie. Since they married a year ago, Friday has always been their night.

"Because it's Friday," the head repeats dully.

"Exactly."

He slides his tie from under his collar and hangs it neatly with his other ties on a tie rack, smoothing the material with one hand. The body places the nail file on the bedside table and hikes its nightgown up around its hips.

As Finn bobs above the body, a stoic expression on his face, the head notices that he keeps twisting his neck around to look at it resting in the chair. Not once does he look at the body. When head and body were attached, the head thought Finn was sweet for staring into her eyes while labouring above the body. But tonight, witnessing the obvious discomfort to his neck, suspicion takes seed and grows. Why won't he look at the body? What is wrong with it?

The body pushes him away.

"Come on now. We were almost finished there." Finn

clears his throat a few times and his eyes are glassy. The sharp point of his Adam's apple twitches along his thin neck.

He still will not look at the body. Dogged by panic, the head asks, "Is the body normal?" Finn has looked upon and touched hundreds of women, seen right up inside them, more than a woman can do herself. Perhaps the body doesn't measure up, aesthetically.

He clears all expression from his face, as the head imagines he does with his patients, and looks at the body. He puts his hand up inside of it. "I'm feeling your cervical walls," he says. The head nods, but the body feels nothing – its cervix numb. With his other hand, he is palpating the skin of the abdomen. His hand is cold and he smiles as if they are sharing some tremendous secret, some depraved and thrilling foreplay. "And I can tell your bladder is almost full." Only then does the head realize it is.

The body lies on his hand like a hand puppet.

"Absolutely normal." Finn smiles as he clambers back on top of it.

Only somewhere far away, in some deep cleft of bone, is there a slight protest. The head stares at the closed curtains on the window, recollecting the finer points of marriage. When they met at university in the city and she was flunking out, having changed her degree from geology to palaeontology to architecture, he seemed not to care, he seemed to regard her presence in his life only with a sweet gratitude, looking amazed when she took his hand in public. He had not dated many women, he said. Both of them were so grateful for the other's interest; gratitude was the overriding sentiment of their courtship. Other feelings, the forces of attraction, took subordinate roles. She dropped out of university, married him, and they moved to this squalid, isolated suburb on the escarpment.

Now, a year later, the head glances at the bed and catches Finn staring towards it.

The body pushes him away.

"It hurts," the head says, which is true. Sharp fiery pains have begun again just under the belly button, and the head feels them zinging through its hypothalamus.

"This thing, it's not real," Finn mutters petulantly.

And then he says the words that he would never dare say to his patients.

"It's all in your head."

What he means is that the pain is *merely* in the head, and not anywhere in the body. He means that the head is lying. The head opens its mouth but is without words. Why are there no words?

It pinches its lips tightly closed again. It should not have to apologize; the lab found blood. Its excuse is airtight.

When the head and body were connected, the head had been bossy and domineering. Now, without its supervision, the body falls back upon primeval skills to navigate the streets and sidewalks that lead to the specialists' offices. It is a strange kind of seeing that the body does without the head. A sensual awareness. A bone-knowing. Sensations from the outside world travel along nerve axons as thundering forms and liquid shapes: a breeze hitting the arm communicates the size of a person walking past; vibrations from the ground, their subtle boom-bahs or ticker-tickers, pass through the feet and paint a picture of a whole streetscape – buildings, cars, traffic lights. Thank goodness it is summer and the body can leave its arms and legs bare. It no longer sleeps under suffocating covers at night either. They make the body feel as the head would if someone wrapped a wet cloth around its eyes, ears and nose.

At the hospital, the specialists perform an ultrasound on the aching pelvis. They beam radiation at it, take samples from it, send tubes through it, shoot saline solutions into it and then simply shake their heads over it. The body spends a lot of time on its back, surrounded by strangers; the head would be mortified. But even after all the attention, the pelvis still flares with pain. Sometimes the pain is a constant dull ache and sometimes it is sporadic and shooting. Sometimes the pain bores through the belly and sometimes it moves towards the hips. Sometimes it seems to be everywhere.

At home, the head reads the specialists' brochures with contempt. What a burden, this body!

The body continues to drag itself to appointments, but the specialists are stymied, so they close their file folders and say that they've done all they can.

At home, head and body sit down together, grudgingly, and write a note, the head dictating to the hand. The hand writes, "But what about intimacy? What should I do about

pain during intimacy?" The head had found this euphe-
mism in a brochure.

When the body places the note in front of one of the
specialists, during their final appointment together, his
right eyelid develops a tic, which the body experiences as
a moist flickering and fluttering vibration against its skin.
The flicker-flutter goes on for minutes. Finally, the special-
ist takes out a pen and writes something on the bottom of
the note.

At home, the head reads his words out loud. "Don't
worry. You can still have children. This thing won't affect
your reproductivity."

"Otherwise, if it hurts, just don't be intimate, or be
intimate as little as possible."

The head orders the body to turn the note over, but the
other side is blank.

In the worsening war between head and body, the head
is the aggressor. It bombards the body with morose
thoughts, insults and catcalls, sometimes pestering the
body into such nervous confusion that it spends minutes
walking again and again into a wall while the head looks
leeringly on. Unlike the head, the body is not malicious
or plotting, but simply as clumsy and thoughtless as a
furry moth at night. It sets the head down face first and
then forgets to move it for hours. One morning it places
the head, precariously, recklessly, on the closed lid of the
toilet while taking a shower. The head stews and fumes.
What is to prevent it from rolling off its slippery perch

and cracking against the ceramic floor tiles? After this, the head ceases communication. Before there was a hum of connection, a moving energy, as though the head were commanding the body from afar, over a shortwave radio. Now, there is only an angry static fuzz. And without some command from the head, the body has trouble. Its bone-knowing goes only so far. It hops onto the wrong buses, or hops onto the right buses but gets off at the wrong stops. It is helpless against two Jehovah's Witnesses on the street, who back it against a mailbox because it cannot talk its way around them.

Finn is losing patience. Every week, he becomes more anxious. Every week, more restless and at odds with his body in the house, pacing and pulling at the plant leaves. On the fourth Friday, he comes home from work and walks into the bedroom, where the body, naked from the waist up, is folding laundry and looking for a clean sweatshirt. Sheets, towels and underwear lie across the bed and the ironing board stands by the window. The head is tumbled together with a clean pile of sheets in the laundry basket on the floor, where the body placed it for safekeeping.

Finn looks at the ironing board, at the littered bed, at the hours of folding and ironing ahead of them. He looks down reproachfully at the head.

"You don't understand what you're asking me to give up. It is very hard for a man . . ." This sounds like something he might have heard in an old movie, muttered around a cigarette by a wooden-faced actor. He lowers his voice and tries to glower menacingly at the head, but his delicate fingers, fidgeting with his pant legs, tremble like butterfly wings.

Of course both head and body understand what he has given up. Haven't they given it up too? Muffled by clean sheets, the head cannot say a word, so the body turns suddenly to Finn, filled with their shared loss. Its arms reach out and its heavy breasts swing through the air, catching Finn off guard. On his surprised, unprepared face, the head sees an expression of fear.

And then pure aversion.

The shock of seeing this expression passes through both head and body like an underwater sound – a subdued, dull boom in a water tank. It resonates with an existing knowledge, already in the bones, and the head closes its eyes. Does Finn really believe that they have given up anything? Hasn't this illness just offered them a convenient excuse?

A fiery pain slams through the body, causing it to buckle at the abdomen. It fumbles for a clean t-shirt and covers itself.

Distrust spreads like a rank mould along the body's arteries. It no longer buys the head's apparent detachment. And even the head, for all its previous denials, must admit how the pain would look to an outsider or to a jury. It would look suspicious. After holding out for so long, the head begins to doubt itself.

The body carries the head off to a head doctor, who has a white moustache and a small wart on his nose.

"Is it possible that this pelvic problem is really in my

head?" asks the head from a leather club chair in front of the doctor's knees.

The doctor nods sagely and asks about seismic events from the head's childhood. He wants to know its dreams. He informs it that dreams about desire are not about desire, they are about parents, dead family pets, a best friend from grade three. Except that the head is pretty sure the dreams are just about desire, nightly nudges from the body reminding the head of something it had enjoyed in the past.

"We're getting off track," the head explains. "It's not that complicated. It's mostly about the chemistry. My husband doesn't smell like anything to me, and he once told me that he thinks I smell like fried vegetables."

But this is no explanation, the doctor says, smirking fondly. It is too simple and not how women work, thinking only of the pleasure in their bodies. His moustache shivers and wriggles above his lips. Unlike the other doctors, who will not treat the head, this doctor refuses to contemplate the body. He barely looks at where it sits impatiently in the corner, tapping its foot. They were hostile to one another from the beginning. The head knew this when the body refused to shake the doctor's hand.

The doctor says to the head, "It's a conversion disorder. You've manifested this phantom pain so you can avoid sleeping with your husband."

Conversion disorder simply sounds to the head like a new term for hysteria. It sounds a lot like what Finn thinks.

The head asks, "But what about the sharp pains, what about the blood?"

The head doctor frowns and scowls down at his papers as he shuffles through them. "Blood?" He picks up a pink sheet with trembling hands. "Blood?"

The left side of his face falls slack, as though he's suffered a sudden stroke.

"You need to take that to your other doctors," he barks through the right side of his mouth.

He dismisses the head. There is the blood, he reminds it, as though to excuse his failure. The problem cannot be all in the head. Wherever it started, it is now in the body.

He doesn't stand up, and his left arm lies across his desk like a slab of raw meat.

Head and body have exhausted the possibilities of separate treatment. It is time to find that no man's land, uninhabited by the doctors, that lies somewhere between head and body. It is time to reconnect.

When head and body arrive home, they sense small absences. Empty spaces hang in the coat closet, and the red pattern on the mat in the front hall, normally covered by Finn's shoes, is now visible. Only the phone table, where the wedding pictures stand, seems unaffected. The photos are among the few things Finn has not touched in leaving.

With Finn gone from the house, the head and body breathe more easily. They no longer spend Friday nights tense and rigid, preparing for a fight, and remembering a time when they did not barricade themselves against Finn, they let their guards down around each other.

Together, they start attending yoga classes and going

for long walks. The body appreciates the head's guidance, and the head enjoys being taken out again and seeing the world. Not only does the body benefit from the exercise, with tighter muscles and brisker circulation, but the head receives soothing endorphins from the body, which dampen pain signals from the abdomen. At night, when the pain in the pelvis begins to hum through the nerves, the head and body practise deep breathing – the head sniffing deeply and the body pushing air down through the chest and into the lungs. The body places a soothing hand on the abdomen and the head murmurs, "There, there. It's okay. Do what you need to do."

Relishing their growing partnership, head and body concoct a plan. With the head resting precariously on the dashboard of the car, giving orders, the body drives down the escarpment to the office of a new doctor. In the parking lot, the body lays the head, grinning with collusion, at the bottom of a canvas bag and then tops the bag with bakery rolls and a bunch of grapes. Once the office door is closed and the doctor is sitting down, the body reaches into the bag and, with the cunning of a flasher, withdraws the head. The head immediately starts to speak.

"Are you sure this pain is not a little in my head and a little in my body? Look, look!" The head sits like a bomb on the doctor's desk. A talking bomb. "Just a bit? Maybe twenty-eighty? Thirty-seventy?" At this point, the head is willing to bargain.

The doctor is young, and his sepia skin shines with

oil, which makes him look ruddy and enthusiastic. He shows no nervousness at the sight of the head. In fact, he even smiles kindly into its eyes. But as the head describes the pain, a dry, nervous cough begins in the doctor's throat. Even so, he manages to say, "People carry stress in different places. Maybe you keep yours in your abdomen."

Both body and head get excited. The head imagines the uterus and bladder as little purses or denim pockets, containing the lint and crumbs of daily emotions. The body throws the head into the doctor's lap, and the head says, "Let's talk about that. Let's talk about why I put my stress there. I have a few ideas."

It rolls forward into the doctor's crotch, pinning him to his chair.

The head talks while the doctor listens and coughs.

When the head stops speaking, the doctor looks down into the eyes, where they regard him from his lap, and spreads wide his arms in helplessness.

He leans forward, whispers a word, and then his voice trails off.

"Pardon?" asks the head.

"Hysteria . . ." and with one tremendous, rasping cough, the doctor seems finally to clear his throat ". . . is no longer something doctors talk about. I have no language for your problem."

"We need a new language," the head says.

Neither head nor body wants to go back in time. They must move past that word – with its tone of condescension and dismissal – but it cannot be ignored either. Certain things must be said to move forward.

For the first time, the room is quiet. The doctor's cough, silenced.

Somehow, the doctor is looking at the head in his lap and past it to the body at the same time. Seen through this gaze, body and head feel a slow, steady dissolution begin. An unravelling of separateness. And all those pronouns that were lost – *she, her* – return to her brain and swim through her blood. Oh, how they had all fallen away from her during this sickness. For so long it had been only the head, or only the body. For so long she had been unable to locate herself anywhere. For where was *she*, where did that single person exist, with head and body divided? But now, now all the lost words return.

"Why don't you tell me what your biggest problem is?" the doctor seems to croon into her ear in his now clear voice. "Tell me how you're sick."

And just like that, something dark and aching moves through head and body simultaneously. It surges up from the depth of a bone and coheres into an idea of words. In the doctor's lap, her head opens its sad eyes and opens its mouth and says the words.

"I miss sex," her head says.

Then both head and body are too sad to even move.

She doesn't miss sex with Finn, but before Finn.

She remembers how the sight of a stranger's bent head, the thin tendons running up the back of a neck, made her dizzy with desire, caused her stomach to drop and her

vision to blur. She remembers the bounding, doglike en-
thusiasm that other men brought to sex, the entanglement
of warm hands and mouths and legs and the final flush that
lasted hours and hours into sleep, flooding body and brain.
How had she forgotten? How had she left behind this part
of herself, the part of her before Finn? But she knows the
answer. She chose to leave it behind. She chose to forget
it to save her marriage. And now she is remembering – as
though conjugating the verb of a new language – her desire.
I desire, she desires.

The doctor does not escort her body and head from his
office. Instead, he nods in sympathy and says, "We'll work
on that. I don't know what you have, but you can keep
coming back until we figure it out. Until you are healed."

Then he plucks her head from his lap and replaces it
on her neck.

In the car ride home, the pain in her pelvis starts up.
It is exactly the same but not exactly the same because her
perception of its magnitude has changed. It is now manage-
able. And this makes all the difference.

When Alisa gets home, she finds Finn sitting in their back-
yard on the top step of the wooden deck, staring out across
the fields and housing divisions spread around their little
ridge of land.

"So you're back," she says.

He looks at her, runs his eyes over her reconnected
head and body. "You too."

She sits down beside him. Suddenly, she can find every

word she needs. There seems to be an easy, instant connection between her mouth and where she finds the words, deep in her bones.

"Why are you with me if you're not even attracted to me?"

He rests his forehead on his arms and begins to cry.

His voice sounds as though it is crossing to her over a large distance. "Umm, it's not something I'm good at. I mean, I don't think I've ever been attracted to anyone, really."

She doesn't know what this means, except that there is a story here waiting to be told, and a sorrow in the story. During their marriage, she had expected Finn to look at her body. She never paid much attention to his. But watching him on the deck, the slumped curve of his back, she sees that his body, like her own, carries a history. It bears marks.

Finn raises his head from his arms and looks out across the land below. Only as he begins to speak does Alisa apprehend for the first time the many forces – the glaciers and rivers and wind and frost – that carved the escarpment from the land, that for millions of years eroded the earth and chiselled cliff faces from rock. Her health has turned out to be so much larger than she believed it to be. It does not begin and end with her body, but includes the bodies around her body – the body of her husband, the bodies that have come into contact with his body and even the bodies of the doctors. All these colliding bodies, pushing and shoving each other into what they are.

Games

Woman Alone

The man must stand in my bedroom.

He is here to repair my mattress. I bought it as a new mattress when I was dating the poet and now, still under warranty, it sounds like an old mattress, creaking and whining in response to the slightest movement. I imagine the growing fatigue of my downstairs neighbours, kept awake each night by my restless, lonely thrashings across the squealing bed. How they must dislike me! When I see these neighbours in the stairwell of our apartment building in the daytime, I feel sure that they eye me with a baleful loathing.

Certainly, the mattress is broken. Possibly, the mattress is beyond repair.

The repair man must sit down beside me on the mattress so only five inches of space separate us. He must push into the mattress repeatedly with his hands and, together, we must bounce up and down. The groans and squeaks of faulty springs echo through the bedroom. "Yes," he says. "Yes, this is not a good mattress. I can take care of this."

His plump, hairy hands nestle into the quilted diamonds of the mattress like pregnant spiders.

I must sing out, "Oh, thank you!" with awed delight and clasp my own hands in front of my chest. I must try to make my guttural voice higher and even flutey, if possible.

This is the game I am playing and it has certain rules.

Never mind that the repair man is stout and a grey thatch of hair sprouts from under the back of his collar. Never mind that I am only twenty-nine and he looks to be in his fifties, with purplish pouches under his eyes and the smell of day-old cigar smoke on his breath. Never mind these things. Only his words matter to the game – "I can take care of this."

They imply that his only wish, his fondest desire, is to help me solve the problem that plagues me. Not because it is his job, but because he is a man and I am the special woman for whom he would be willing to solve all problems. These include carrying my groceries home by myself, walking dizzily to the pharmacy when I am sick and phoning the police when the crack addict who lives across the street starts screaming and throwing bottles from his balcony. The repair man must appear, for the twenty minutes of his visit, as though he might do all those things with an easy smile and a jaunty unwillingness to be surprised. And, most important, in the face of each he would say exactly what he has said, "I can take care of this." And with these words I would feel the weight of being vigilant about life slip, momentarily, from my chest.

I must set the alarm every night and resist the urge to sleep and sleep and sleep through the morning or to remain in my bedroom all day, listening to the radio.

The mattress repair man goes down on his knees in front of me, so I can see the grey curls wreathing the bare patch of skin on the crown of his head. He must look up at me – Are his eyes, in fact, twinkling? Yes they are! – and say, "I think I know what the problem is here," as he slides his hand between the box spring and mattress underneath me.

I imagine the neighbours hearing the groaning springs and wondering why I am home every day and seem not to work. Why I cannot ever give them a moment's peace. They do not know that since the poet left I have worked from home, editing high school textbooks. I arrange and rearrange words all day. I hunch over my desk, thumb through dictionaries and almanacs, fuss over the rules of grammar and style, roll and re-roll sentences around on my tongue, make a decision and then change my mind and then change it back again, latch onto a word and think about it and then think about thinking about it. Sometimes two hours, three hours, pass and I realize that I am staring at the same sentence. I work too slowly these days, working from home. I am losing clients, who say, "You get no work done!" "What did you do to this manuscript? I don't see that you did anything!" They do not see the hours of thinking I did about each word, which is the part I enjoy. It is all a game, with the certainty of its rules, and how I enjoy my little games! Ha ha.

Ha ha ha ha ha ha ha ha ha ha ha ha!

"Oh, okay. I see what the problem is. Exactly what I thought."

I must lower my eyes, smiling shyly, slyly, as I feel the movements of the repair man's hand burrowing beneath me.

I must remember to be neat when I leave my apartment. I must not wear the same fraying pair of jeans for five days in a row. I must not sniff my shirts to check whether they smell clean to me but must wash them after every wear. I must not start talking to myself or to pieces of my furniture, the blinds, for instance, asking them how it feels to look upon the outside world every day and, in turn, to be seen every day by the outside world.

And now the repair man must grin, bob his head and slide his hand out from beneath me as he says, modestly, "I'll just get you a new mattress from the truck." The easiest remedy. But offered up like a gift that he hopes I will accept.

And I must stand up and say, "Really? You could do that for me? That is just marvellous!" Never mind that the warranty guarantees the company will provide this service.

But already he has slid the mattress off the box spring and upended it, holding it in the broad span of his arms with pride. I must say, "Can you carry it all by yourself? All the way down the three flights?"

And he must say in a generous and amused voice,

"What, three flights? That's no problem," as he begins to carry-drag the mattress across the floor.

Never mind that just the other day I built my own bookshelves, lifted heavy planks and banged them together by myself, no easy feat. But today, the bookshelves against the walls, filled with books arranged in alphabetical order by author, I forget my own abilities. See how quickly he flips the mattress around and manoeuvres it through the open door into the hallway! Who could imagine such a thing! Such a surprising and otherworldly act of strength.

I must applaud.

He must bow and gesture with two fingers near his forehead, as though tipping an imaginary cap towards me.

I must not get too paranoid when I leave my apartment. I must remember that my clothes are clean and try not to think about things I cannot see or know about myself — a fallen hem at the back of my skirt, a garlicky odour, an odd jerkiness (or smoothness) to my walk. I must remember that when people talk in low voices behind me, there is some chance it is not about me. Once, when I was with the poet at the lake — that limitless, unbounded vista of blue — a lone gull with a crippled wing flew weavingly out across the water, where the other gulls attacked it.

And back my man comes, as he must. Lurching stoically up the stairs, embracing a new mattress wrapped in clear plastic, whistling — whistling! Oh, he is very good at this game. He removes the plastic, slings the mattress into my bedroom and hefts it across the box spring. Then he must slap his hands against the front of his legs and exclaim,

"All done," while looking remarkably pleased with himself and me. He must pat the new mattress and say, "Try it out."

I must look at his patting hand, one of a pair of hands that go out and about in the world. These hands grasp the objects of their trade with confidence and swing tools through the air. I must not think about the poet and how his words were like these hands that connect to the outside world and make things happen there. How if the poet wrote about an ordinary object he found beautiful, when I next looked at it, it was beautiful. How his spontaneous, unstudied words about me during an improvisational poetry reading caused us to grope one another in a cab after the reading, which started a whole sequence of events.

But I must not think about the poet. I must look at the repair man, with his hands patting my mattress. It is as though his hands draw energy from things they touch. Without these things, the hands might die. The hands might wither on the ends of the arms. Or grow cold and clumsy and stupid, as my hands have grown, always clutching at the same book or pen for hours. Always cramping and twitching.

On the street, I must not look at the hands of others. The hands of women and men, or men and men, or women and women. When people walk together, their hands often reach towards one another and intertwine like vines. Or the hand of one will move across the hair or shoulders of the other.

I must not look at these hands.

I must lie back on the mattress. The mattress repair

man must lie beside me. We must rock back and forth. We must jounce our hips up and down. The mattress does not make a sound. "Perfect!" I cry. "Perfect!" he mimics and we grin at one another as though we are children discovering a new wonder – a beetle with an effervescent shell crawling across a beach.

A woman alone, I must not keep alcohol in my apartment.

I must sit up.

I must reach into my wallet and pull out two twenties for the visit, and a ten for his trouble. He must pocket the money and leave.

All games need their rules; otherwise, everything might slide away and fall into nothing.

By Analogy

I know I should marry the yogourt maker. But first I should pick up the phone, dial his apartment and invite him to a movie, for we have never gone on a date and met only once, last year, at a book launch. After the movie, I will think up some intelligent things to say because he is a tenured professor with full benefits (the yogourt-making is merely a hobby). If intelligent thoughts desert me during the evening, as often happens, I will ask him instead how he makes yogourt in those mysterious glass cylinders that he told me line the shelves of his fridge. I will ask if he ever planted the vegetable garden he was planning or if he still bakes himself a pot roast every Sunday night. While he answers my questions, I will be charmed by the way he slips deferential compliments into conversation, as he did at the launch, such as "I remain your obedient servant" or "I accede to your wisdom, Madame Editor." He will say things like this not only to me, but also to the woman selling tickets at the movie theatre and the waitress who will later serve us coffee. He will make us all feel appreciated in different ways, and not the least bit jealous, with his face as open and honest as a thumbtack.

But how is a face as open or honest as a thumbtack? There is no rightness to this pairing, no searing point of connection between the yogourt maker's face and a tack. As an analogy, it is nonsense.

And, truly, the yogourt maker and I would be a nonsensical couple. Walking along the street, he looming a full foot taller, we would look like co-workers who had met up awkwardly, accidentally, and were then forced by politeness to walk together and make conversation. Also, judging from his behaviour at the book launch, he seeks out fit Germanic women, the kind who enjoy camp-outs and canoe trips as he does. So what would he do with me and my indulgences? How could he respond to the caustic remarks I would forever be muttering into his good, trusting face? What could he say, his economical heart sinking within him, when he came home one night to discover me eating a whole store-bought cake from its aluminum package?

And what would I say if I bumbled into the kitchen in the first light of morning and found him lining up his tiny cylinders of yogourt, performing his strange alchemy? My visit to the kitchen would be merely to stave off hunger, to bite some cheese directly off the brick or shove a piece of bread into my mouth, before treading back to bed. But there would be the yogourt, bottle after bottle, neat and white and plain.

So I will leave us in the kitchen – him looking at my yellowing, frayed nightshirt, me contemplating the yogourt, our expressions thick and baffled – and return to the thumbtack. Something has come from this sloppy analogy after all. Some truth. When I think of the yogourt maker alone, himself, he has rightness, but when I try to put us together, he does not, like his honest face and the tack. And I must pay attention to this failed analogy, these words that reach for one another and fall short. In matters of love, I know that bad analogies serve as bad omens, forecasting disaster. I learned this lesson already from the sketch comic.

I know I should not marry the sketch comic. We dated briefly and have agreed to date no longer. At night, he performs his comic routines in clubs, but during the day, to earn money, he works as a typesetter in a publishing house. It is a quiet and sedate publishing house, so when I returned an edited manuscript there six months ago and found him wearing plastic eyeballs over his own, he seemed like a good idea.

All along his bedroom walls are shelves with boxes marked "props" or "wigs" or "glasses"; he has thirty-two pairs of glasses alone. Over time, the wigs have crept from their boxes into the corners of his room, resting on heaps of clothing or uncoiling glossy tentacles from under the bureau. Because his comic sketches are each only a few minutes long, he needs the props and wigs and glasses as a shorthand for larger things. For instance, if he carries a bottle onto the stage, the audience knows he is an alcoholic. If he wears delicate half-glasses on the end of his nose, the audience knows he is a librarian, especially if he holds a book in one hand. I could write this down using the kind of analogy found on exams: glasses are to librarian as bottle is to alcoholic.

My problem with the sketch comic when we were dating was that I did not trust such analogies would hold. Part of his job as a sketch comic was to put things together that should not be together. He pretended to be a librarian in a strip joint or a stripper in a library. He sang a song by a rock singer in the voice of a famous folk singer. So how could I trust that his prop glasses meant he was a librarian? Why did I not think that on such a person the glasses might mean starlet or sea captain?

My growing unease led to an awkward moment when it came time to use a certain word, if it was going to be used at all. This word could feature as the answer to the following analogy: proposal is to marriage as *blank* is to forever. But with the sketch comic, how could I be sure such logic still applied? That if he said that word, in his mind he wouldn't be wearing a wig while he said it? How could I be sure that the word meant to him what it meant to me? That it was analogous to the same things?

So instead of either of us saying anything when we should have, there was only silence. Even then, I knew that when problems of analogy arise between a couple, the end is sure to follow. I had learned my lesson already from the poet.

I know I will not marry the poet. The man I wanted to marry. Or thought I wanted to marry.

It was the misinterpreted and misplaced analogies that did us in, that rankled and precipitated the final betrayal. I developed a series of bladder infections, which he read metaphorically as an emotional recoil from sex with him. And perhaps they were, as I had worked up an eight-month sulk in response to a poem he wrote about me. A poem with me as moody and unpredictable as the weather (a predictable and solid metaphor, to be sure, for a woman, the weather). But I believed the poet was lamenting his own moody and unpredictable feelings for me. He wrote poems about other women, and love with them was a gentle unmooring or an emergence into a summer night.

When he moved to another city, things really got out of hand. I said on the telephone that he could live as he liked, do as he liked, because I trusted him and was no longer jealous. What I meant was that I was miserable and wished he would stop doing as he liked. The poet did not hear what I meant but rather something else entirely that made him cross and wounded. So he slept with someone else and told me about it a few days later. And perhaps I too misinterpreted. Perhaps he meant, "Come back, come back," not "Go away." But by this point we had strayed from analogy completely, our words not at all illuminating our meanings but clouding them, until we could no longer find our way back to analogy or each other.

The night the poet was leading home another woman, I realized later, was the very same night I met the yogourt maker. And because he knew that the poet and I were a couple, he said of me while introducing me to someone else, "Meet so-and-so's better half," and with this analogy I was on solid ground. It was as predictable and sturdy as he was. (And a fine example of his tireless gallantry!) You barely had to think about the expression, a whole made up of two parts. How I approved his use of analogy. I thought, here is a man I could hang my hat on or put my boots under. Here is a man I could marry. But of course, now I think about it, the very fact that I was looking at other men during the book launch meant that his analogy was faulty to begin with. Obviously, I was no longer one part of a whole. Especially since, at that very moment, my other half was possibly raising a suggestive eyebrow or turning back covers or washing out his armpits in a grimy basin in anticipation. We were, in contrast to the yogourt maker's analogy, as separate as we could be.

And this brings me back to the beginning, back to bad analogies, which are really just pairs of words that are uneasily married or not married at all. Between them stretch wide spaces filled with uncertainty, misunderstanding and doubt. And if mere words are so riskily conjoined, what hope is there for two people?

I know I will not marry the yogourt maker.

The Question

I am waiting for the poet to call or send an email in response to my email where I asked him a specific question. I have waited one week. Only three reasons for his delay suggest themselves to me. Some of these reasons are forgivable and some are less forgivable, so here I am *again* in relation to the poet, asking myself what I can forgive and where the limits of forgiveness fall. (But certainly that does not bear thinking about right now – his earlier betrayal. Why think about it? I will put it from my thoughts. My mind needs to sort out this more immediate problem of forgiveness.)

The first reason for the poet's delayed response, which I could forgive completely, is that he has not yet read my question. He might have retreated to his trailer on the northern lake, for instance, and cannot access his email. If this is the case, he will return home days or weeks from now, read my question for the first time and rush to the phone to call me and apologize with an outpouring of words. He will also give me his answer, and when I imagine this scenario his answer is always the one most pleasing to me. In fact, while on retreat, he will have written a clutch of love poems for me. His straightforward, spontaneous words will affect easy change in our situation: they will transform the world into a beautiful place, as they have always done. I will cry and forgive his delayed response with no reservations and a sudden lifting of the weight in my stomach. I will forgive him all the more because I brought the disaster upon myself, emailing him a garbled, hesitant sentence instead of trying to talk to him in person or on the phone; however, I can never get him in person or on the phone, and truthfully I wanted a bit of time between my question and his response — time for predictions and anticipations and hypotheses. Anyway, it is decided: for this delay, I would grant him full forgiveness.

A second reason for his delay — which I could forgive but with reservation, as though I had caught the wiggle of centipede legs from the corner of one eye — is that he has read my question but become paralyzed by the terror born of love. I am not being immodest, I think, when I say that he displays the nervous tics of affection when we meet. The first time we met, accidentally, after he moved back to this city a month ago, he darted into a public restroom and left me standing with my arm raised in greeting. One day, I cornered him in the park near his apartment, against a picnic table, but he pretended to be in a great rush to get somewhere, too rushed to give me more than a quick nod. In fact, it is hard to get him alone; he seems to be always moving away from me or not answering his phone when I call. But now he is caught! Now he has read my question and worries, as before an interview for a long-sought job, about his potential for success. Especially as we failed together once before. I know that if fear is the reason for his delay but he masters this fear and manages to answer my question, with many stops and starts, his words will aggravate me, as much as I may want to forgive them, because their hesitancy indicates anxieties about me that will resurface at our most intimate moments, causing awkward bedroom scenes with sudden withdrawals and fast retreats and him pulling sheets up to his neck and me hunching gracelessly into my clothes while crying. So although I would forgive him a delay due to fear, I would do so with a feeling of reluctant foreboding.

The third reason for his delay in responding to my email, which I would try to forgive before failing, is that he has read my question but is already involved with another woman. Because he no longer cares for this woman, he delays his response to me, thinking, *Perhaps if I break things off quickly with this first woman, I can move back to this other woman, so I will not answer until I know my situation.* Certainly, I do not know his situation. The truth is that I never asked, nor did I look at his ring finger. Nor have I asked anyone of our mutual acquaintance what happened during the two years since we parted. I have seen him twice at his local supermarket with a red-headed woman, but they might have been friends. It was hard to confirm this, standing as I was behind baskets of apples and then the leaves of potted ferns. I could not hear a word he said to her, he was whispering so close to her ear, but quite surely they were friends. Friends do whisper and tease and sometimes even link arms, and it doesn't mean anything. In fact, a friend might serve as a sort of surrogate when one is pining for someone else. But if I am wrong and he is with the red-headed woman, he will leave her for me after a painful emotional struggle, perhaps pulling me forcefully into his arms with only an inarticulate grunting. How wordless our passions make us, especially in situations like these! So I know that I should forgive him for his delayed response in this situation, even though his leaving of one woman for another will bring up discomforting memories for me, which are best left unremembered. Unfortunately, months into things, I will be looking at him with his female friends and wondering what words he is saying to them. Or rifling through his desk drawers in search of love poems about other women. Or sliding my hand into his pants pockets when he is in another room, looking for love notes addressed to him. It will become apparent that while I forgave him for his delay, I did not forgive his wronging of the other woman. That will be very hard to forgive.

Of course, a cynic might suggest another reason for the poet's delay, which I entertain here only to explore the paradoxical boundaries of forgiveness. A cynic might say that the poet read my question and then forgot that I asked it. It meant so little to the poet that it slipped his mind completely. (And again the discomforting un-memories stir about murkily. How strange it would be to find myself in that situation with the poet again! So like that other unmentionable situation, where he never sought my forgiveness because by then, to him, I was insignificant.) The cynic would point out that if I was to see the poet on the street a year from now and smile graciously and say, "I forgive you," the poet would say nothing and look only baffled. My forgiveness, undesired and unsought, would be irrelevant to him. And I find, paradoxically, that this would be most unforgivable.

The Odious Child

The child is restless. I brace myself.

It gambols through the apartment, thick nails scraping the hardwood. It breaks the safety latch on the fridge and rips open a package of raw chicken breasts. Chicken fat splatters against the white ceramic floor tiles. By the time I wet a sponge, three chicken breasts are gone. I send the child to the living room, so I can wash the kitchen floor, and there it leaps from the couch to the coffee table, again and again, hooting with excitement. Glass coasters fly onto the floor. The floor lamp vibrates and totters. The child tears off its diaper and scrapes its bum repeatedly across the arms of the couch, as though scratching an itch. Streaks of brown stain the pale green silk upholstery. By the time I get to the living room with the upholstery shampoo, the child is sniffing and licking those same filthy streaks. I shriek and banish it to the corner. It moves on all fours – not on hands and knees as a normal human child would, crawling, but on hands and feet, its bum the top of an awkward triangle.

From the corner, I hear a low-pitched groaning, softer than the child's usual ebullient barks. It has straddled my moccasin, grinding into it. I cry out and flail my hands, not wanting to touch the child performing this repugnance. Eventually, I take up my umbrella and prod the child away from the slipper, into the study at the far end of the apartment. It goes, with many growls and mournful backward glances at its beloved.

And just as I am shutting the child behind the study door, it reaches up its arms to me.

I set right the apartment and make my usual Saturday breakfast – one boiled egg. While I eat, I pick strands of the child's pale brown fur off my linen skirt and place them on a napkin.

I can only imagine what the apartment would become if I let the child free and left – a soiled den of masturbation. It is fortunate I am here to restrain it.

Oh, how I loathe it.

In an earlier century, people would have called the child "feral" and given some wondrous account of its origin, of how it emerged from a forest or ravine after being raised by wolves. I have read such accounts, the journals of worthy and curious doctors who found feral children and attempted to understand them through education. There is minor progress, the child eating with a spoon for instance, and learned discourses on what makes one human and the relationship between wilderness and civilization. But what can wilderness mean to me, here in this city?

The view from my kitchen reveals a parkette bounded by four busy streets.

And although there are similarities between my child and its feral ancestors – yes, the child is covered in pale brown fur, and yes, its eyes glow with a blue intensity in the dark, and yes, it groans and shrieks, rather than vocalizing anything close to speech – I have never tried to civilize or understand the child, and I have no interest in reflecting upon its origins (although, certainly, I did not give birth to it). We so rarely understand ourselves, let alone others.

My responsibility, my burden, since discovering the child is to keep it hidden, not broadcast its existence. Civility demands this. No civilized person would want to know about the child, and I take my responsibilities to others seriously.

For some reason I cannot explain, the thought of a slip, of someone seeing the child, mortifies me.

I fold the napkin around the fur once and once again.

There is a knock at my door.

I remain calm although I hear a scuffle and thump from the study. The child has been alarmed by the noise.

I look through the peephole and see the neighbour.

Concerns bind my heart.

The neighbour is a round and smiling young woman, who no doubt looks at every stranger with this same expectation of pleasure. Two pairs of combat boots stand in the hall outside her apartment door, and she is forever tromping past my own door on her way to the stairwell. I overhear her in the hallways hallooing to the other tenants, who are as quiet and unnoticeable as I am. At the moment, I cannot even recollect their faces.

Until now I have avoided the neighbour, for I have never had one before and do not know how to behave (her apartment was converted from a utility room). If I pretended I did – rushed her with gifts, or greeted her with a hearty shout, or smiled – my inept attempts at these things would illustrate my ignorance, so although I spy on her through the peephole, I ignore her in the hallways. Let her think me a busy and distant neighbour but a neighbour nonetheless, rather than an incompetent who knows nothing of neighbourliness.

But today! Her knock is not a request but a command that cannot be ignored.

I imagine the child is cowering in the study. We rarely have visitors, and I have learned to fix appliances and electrical problems myself for fear of someone seeing the child. In fact, my fear of someone discovering the peculiar creature has enabled me to become quite self-sufficient, for which I am thankful. As a substitute teacher, often between jobs, I have time to spend on household repairs.

I open the door on the chain and there she is, her lips painted sloppily in bright red, the toes of her boots pointing right at me. She shouts, "Hello neighbour!" She has lipstick on her teeth. "I live next door. I just moved from . . ." and here she names a small northern town. No wonder she is so unusual. No wonder she does not understand the rules of our building. She stuffs a flyer through the crack and says, "I have something for you!" Why is she shouting? How it hurts my ears. When I take the flyer – a piece of unimportant advertising bearing the slogan "Be heard!" – she gives a little bow with her arm still extended as though she is a courtier and I, a princess. To my horror, a barking shriek escapes my mouth, the causes of which I can only attribute to my nervousness that the child will reveal itself. The neighbour grins with pleasure.

At this point, I notice that the child has escaped the study, come up beside me, without a sound, and pushed its furry face into the crack between the door's edge and wall to stare at the neighbour. It would push itself through the crack if it could, inquisitive beast.

The neighbour must not see the child. I could not bear it.

I shut the door without a word.

After she leaves, I worry, for is this not only the beginning? I imagine, from the way she grinned, it is. She will come back.

I pace my apartment while the child groans and plays with its toes. The phone is ringing, but I do not answer it. I keep most of my blinds closed against the surrounding office towers and apartments, except those in the bedroom where nothing looks in. It is impossible we should be discovered by anyone outside the building. But now the neighbour. The neighbour! What a confusing relation, like a cousin once removed or an in-law. It is hard to know just what to do with a neighbour. How close to get.

While I hope to have few dealings with her, the truth is that my life has changed.

I have a neighbour and must prepare. Civility demands it.

First things first – I have grown lazy. From now on, I will keep the child locked in the study at all times.

Always the phone is ringing, and always I am not picking it up. Why can we not be left alone? More advertising slogans on my machine – "Speak out! Keep your rights!" I keep to myself, thank you.

Today in the bathroom mirror, I practise smiling as a neighbour should.

First, I raise one corner of my upper lip, but this is too much like a snarl, so I try raising both corners of my upper lip, slightly. This is the smile I will share with my neighbour. It is civil, but not supplicating, for I neither want nor need anything from her.

In the study, the child begins whining and scrabbling at the wall between my apartment and the neighbour's. I thump on the locked study door with my palm and the scrabbling stops. I suppose I could be more indulgent, but the child needs so much. If indulged, it will only grow more ravenous until it brings the whole apartment down around us.

(Here, I am distracted by some yelling on the street and a siren. I shut the window and turn on the air-conditioning without bothering to lift my blinds. I live between a fire station and police station, and if I looked outside every time a siren sounded, I would spend all day at the window.)

Before I can go back to the mirror, another knock! Accompanied by a repeated clunking sound from the hallway.

The neighbour is at my door, wearing an unzipped backpack filled with flyers. I did not imagine she would knock again so soon. Surprised, I step back from the doorway and she walks a few feet into my apartment. In one hand she carries a megaphone and in the other, a gas mask. She knocks the mask against the megaphone repeatedly, with the merriment of a toddler. I avert my eyes. One does not comment on the personal possessions of one's neighbours.

I try out my smile . . . and give the wrong one. The snarl.

From her, a coy insinuation as she turns her head to look towards the study. "I heard some noises from your apartment earlier. Do you have a pet?"

Slight shake of my head.

"Or a larger animal?" A leering twinkle.

I do not discuss intimacies. I have endured few, rife with the usual hygienic horrors I would rather not contemplate.

"Did you read my flyer about tomorrow afternoon? Are you going?" She shakes her head. "The situation is becoming serious, as I'm sure you know."

Here, success! I manage the proper smile, just as she has stopped smiling.

She says, "Why don't I stop by tomorrow afternoon, so we can go together?"

"Stop by . . . of course. I'll go shopping." Inexplicably, I turn pink. The child turns pink during a difficult bowel movement. I can see the flush under its fur.

She looks confused when I mention shopping but recovers quickly, smashing the mask against the megaphone once more and shouting "See you!" before tromping down the stairs, whistling.

I will throw a wine and cheese party. I've seen them on television and the covers of food magazines.

With shaking hands, I scribble out a grocery list. A person who didn't know better might mistake my industry for excitement.

In the study, the child is going berserk. I hear books toppling from shelves and the wheeled chair rolling over the floor. Even so, I feel confident I will be able to restrain it for the duration of the neighbour's visit.

Shopping takes all afternoon because the only food in the apartment is food the child likes – bananas, bran flakes, carrot sticks, oatmeal and unseasoned meat. Also, an unusual number of shabby men and women crowd the subway, holding signs. I have to push through them to reach the doors.

I buy pale yellow cheeses at a store I've never had reason to enter. The strange little man running the store is hammering boards over the windows when I approach. As I leave, he returns to his hammering and says, "Be careful, humming lady." I do not know what he means, strange little man, so I do not respond. I would never hum in public.

There is going to be a parade of some kind, obviously. Police officers saunter the street in pairs, like dancers in a cotillion. Two policemen stop me outside the store to ask why I am on the street. I suppose such vigilance is normal when you are in charge of a big event. I, too, am in charge of a big event. I explain my business quickly. The policemen and I have much to do, and I can see they appreciate my professionalism.

I wonder what the parade will celebrate. How festive is the world! And tomorrow I am throwing a party! My canvas bag bulges with cheese, grapes and walnuts.

Sometimes I . . . long for the child. Living alone day after day . . . it is not that I am lonely, exactly. When I get home, I stand with my palm on the study door, resting it there. The ornery child is silent, of course. My hand moves to the doorknob. I turn it halfway before remembering to stop.

I am prepared this time for the neighbour's knock.

I have laid the cheese out on a large platter with crackers, pear slices, walnuts and the dark burgundy grapes shining in their skins. I saw such a welcoming vision on the cover of a magazine in the grocery store, the platter surrounded by a group of rosy cheeked people, mouths gaping with laughter. It did not seem . . . unpleasant.

In the early afternoon, I vacuumed and then mopped to remove any stray fur. As I dusted, I watched a television show about a political demonstration because one of the streets with protestors was similar to my very own.

Any personal items, and there were but a few — a newspaper, some mail, a pair of modest pearl earrings, my toothbrush on the bathroom counter — I swept into drawers and cupboards.

It does not bear mentioning how I needed to restrain the child inside the study closet, to ensure its silence for the duration of the visit.

When the neighbour arrives, she looks tired and wears a white bandana over her nose and mouth. She seems confused as she progresses into the living room. There is not much to see! Ha! I have foiled her curiosity. I uncork a Chardonnay and pour glasses for two. I extend the cheese plate, smiling a triumphant smile. Oh, how well I am dissembling! How well I am proving capable of the neighbour game! I watch myself in amazement as though from above.

I will have to speak. I have prepared some remarks although I now realize that I could not prepare for hers.

"So how was your day?"

"My day? The demonstration, you mean?"

"Ah," I say, glad to make a connection, "I was just watching a demonstration show on television."

She pulls the bandana down from her nose and mouth, so it hangs around her neck. Her face is in partial shadow because she has sat on the edge of the couch, just in front of the floor lamp. The shadow on her right cheek is the same colour as the grapes.

"This is not television," she says.

I sense that she wants something from me. I thrust the cheese plate on her, but she ignores it.

It is now that a slight noise from the study begins to concern me.

"We should go down into the street, we should join the others right now, before it's too late. They are being arrested though they have done nothing illegal, or violent. We thought when the time came we had the right to speak out. We thought we did, but when the time came . . ."

She looks at me expectantly. Why should she expect more than my neighbourly ministrations?

I say, "You appear upset. May I get you some ice water?"

She stares at me and says nothing.

Surely, I can hear something from the study? A shuffling rustle, as the child struggles to free itself?

The neighbour leans forward and puts her hand on my leg, just above the knee.

The cheese plate falls from my hands, upending when it hits the edge of the coffee table. Grapes bounce and roll across the table and floor, one landing in my lap. And still her hand remains on my knee. I look into her shadowy face.

She says, "Don't you feel any responsibility, anything at all, for the people outside?"

Oh, the odious child! The horrible noise from the study!

I can no longer bear it. Nor can I bear the neighbour's imploring, incomprehensible stare.

I stand up.

She expects something from me, her hostess. I must give her something. Civility demands it.

"Come," I say.

I move into the hallway and walk towards the study.

She stands up with an anxious smile and follows.

We proceed to the end of the hallway where I throw open the door of the study. When I place my hand on the closet door, I hear a noise although it is not coming from the closet as I expected but from the window, which has been left open a crack. Distracted, I move away from the closet, open the window and stick my head out.

The window looks onto an alleyway on the side of my building. If I turn my head, I can see, between the edge of my building and the building close beside it, one small piece of the street.

It is a dark vision.

Lines of police officers march past in bulky black riot gear, holding clear shields in front of their chests. They are banging these shields with batons, in unison. I smell smoke in the air. I hear whistles and shouts. With the windows closed and the air conditioning on, we heard nothing. Now, I see three black vans creep up behind the last line of officers, their back doors open, and the officers doubling back, throwing struggling civilians into the vans. Four officers drag a woman along the ground, so her head bounces on the asphalt. I cannot say whether she lives on my street.

I shut the window and turn away.

"I had thought to show you something," I say, "but now think better of it."

The neighbour retreats down the hallway, away from me.

With the window shut, I realize how quiet the study is. I open the closet door a crack and peek inside.

The child is gone.

I walk into the closet and then out, and then in again. I look under the desk and behind the chair. I return to the closet. It is easy to see the child is not on the closet shelf while standing beneath it, but even so, I drag over an arm-chair and step onto the seat. Above the shelf, a ventilation grate that I didn't know existed hangs from one hinge, exposing the child-sized mouth of the duct behind it. I do not know whether this is new damage but notice a tuft of downy fur stuck in the grate. The duct itself is dark, and I cannot see more than a few inches into it.

Dazed, I get off the chair and move down the hallway towards the neighbour.

"I need to go," she says impatiently, although she supports herself against the wall.

I let her go.

I do not mention the chaos outside. I was only looking through a narrow opening after all. It is hard to say what I was seeing.

And I don't have the words to ask her to stay. I will never have them.

These days, I leave my blinds open.

There is no longer anything to hide, for the child deserted me on the night of the neighbour's visit. It retreated, it seems, into the deepest fissures of the building, so deep I do not imagine I will see it again.

Some nights, very late, while I lie alone in my bed in the dark, I think I hear muffled metallic rustlings from behind the walls and ceiling. These could be mice, though, or the invisible motions of other tenants. A week ago, another more reserved neighbour moved into the apartment next door. I don't know what happened to the first neighbour, for I did not see her again after that night at my apartment. The new neighbour has never knocked, but we always nod at one another in the halls.

I feel fortunate to share a floor with such a civil neighbour.

During times like this, when I remember the child and everything that happened, I walk into the study and shut the door behind me. The study door is particularly ornate on the outside. It is wood, painted white, with five raised panels. It still has the original brass doorknob, backplate and keyhole, though the key is long lost and the keyhole painted over. The door often stays shut a long while.

Thirty-Seven Women

We were a community of thirty-seven women. Each woman lived alone in one of thirty-seven apartments in our six-storey building.

The tall caretaker with fine manners did not own the building, nor was he the superintendent. The owner and the superintendent were unmannered and squat. They blustered into our apartments without notice and walked through every room without removing their shoes first, as the caretaker always did. They asked how we were managing but left before we could answer, because we might ask them to fix a smoke detector, heft an air conditioner into a window or perform various other favours they did not feel were their responsibilities. They treated us with fearful belligerence as though we, the thirty-seven women, were wild animals who might leap at their throats if not mastered. It was the superintendent who vacuumed the hallways with a round industrial vacuum and who was paid by the owner to fix our plumbing.

The caretaker, on the other hand, was not employed to be in our building as far as we could see. We did not even know whether he lived in the building. He stood in the stairwells and hallways on his stilt-like legs and took care – he held open the front door when we approached with armfuls of groceries, he warned us of ice on the sidewalks, he reminded us that the weatherman promised rain as we dashed recklessly from our apartments, causing us to creep back in and retrieve umbrellas. Often, when we felt neglected by the management of the building, we invited the caretaker into our apartments to listen to our worries about cracks forming on the walls or taps that would not stop dripping. While we complained, he smiled politely. And sometimes he fixed things that the superintendent had not yet fixed – he patched up the cracks with a rusty trowel and some filler, or brought a plastic case of rubber washers into our bathrooms and tended to the taps. He took our cares upon himself, for that was the sort of caretaker he was.

Because the caretaker's manners were so gentle and his pale hair so long, pulled into a ponytail like a woman's, we allowed him to come into our apartments and touch all our things, without a thought. Always we spoke of his fine manners and demure smile, when we spoke of him to one another. He had the nicest manners. The nicest manners of any man we knew. That was the first thing we spoke about when we mentioned the caretaker. "Oh and his lovely manners," we murmured, our voices hushed with reverence. We were thirty-seven women, all with different backgrounds and experiences, but on his lovely manners, we could agree.

At night he made sure we were safe. After we had come home and locked our doors against the night hallways and each other, he walked the hallways, past each door, and we heard his long arms swish-swishing against his yellow t-shirt. It was always the same t-shirt, the colour of the sun in a child's drawing, and it was always as clean and bright as if he'd bought it new that morning. We lay alone in our beds, listening to the sound of him walking past our doorways in that shirt, and it was a ritual that meant the day was over and we could go to sleep.

The thing about him was this: during the whole time he was cleaning up our messes and knocking gently on our doors at three in the morning – just when we were wishing he would knock, just when a toilet had become stuck on a repeated flush – during the whole time he was listening to our fears and watching our lives unravel, he accepted no payment. Not one glass of water after hauling heavy boxes up the stairs, not one homemade cookie or wine bottle with a bow. If we tried to offer him these things he would smile mildly and insist that we keep them for ourselves. We might need them. We would enjoy them more than he. He thought only of us. All we could do in return for his unselfish devotion was thank him and thank him in voices that seemed to grow shrill with nerves and gratitude.

Sundays were the days that we felt some friction, some rub of unpleasantness and discord in our relationship, when he cared for us less than normal. We were a community of women, all living under one roof, and we liked to do our laundry together on Sunday mornings, when we streamed from our building and down the street to the laundromat, prepared to whiten our whites as church bells chimed forth in the blue air. The caretaker stood at the base of the stairs, in the front entranceway, and when we passed he would avert his eyes from our laundry bags. At first, this seemed polite, but it began to wear on us after a while, as though he, in his clean yellow shirt, reproached us for dirtying the towels, sheets and clothing. We began to conceal our dirty laundry in grocery bags or gym bags. One woman took to wrapping dirty laundry in a clean white sheet before putting it into her see-through mesh laundry bag. Perhaps we were imagining the caretaker's distaste, we each reasoned privately. Perhaps he did not like Sundays because we were all out of the building, away from his care. Perhaps that was it, but we knew that he did not like Sundays.

I myself once walked past the caretaker with a load of dirty dishcloths and underwear in my arms. I felt ashamed for mixing the two, for being so unsanitary, although I could not decide whether it was more unsanitary for underwear to be against dirty kitchen things, or kitchen things to be against dirty underwear. In my apartment, throwing the laundry into a bag, I had not felt this shame. I only felt it later, as I passed by the caretaker and his averted gaze. He had such good manners himself, it was hard for him to be around people who dirtied laundry and carried it through the streets. I was not a good person, I thought. Then in my mind I blamed him for this thought.

Not long after the day I laundered my dishcloths and underwear, he disappeared.

At first, the other women and I were more guarded than normal, but after a week or two we became confiding. Phone numbers were exchanged and a steady currency of homemade baking and steaming casserole dishes flowed through the hallways. We even began to take liberties, expecting our knocks to be answered, expecting our calls to be returned. Shareen began whistling on the stairwells, Doris came home drunk one night and lay in a happy trance on the hallway floor, Vanessa received a different man into her apartment every weekend and screamed into the night. Miriam and Lucy moved in together and painted the walls with murals. Doreen, Junie and Sasha built a set of bike racks for the basement. Agnes threw a dinner party for Linda, Augusta and Lulu, after which Linda got severe food poisoning and was driven to the hospital by Denise, and fed soup the next day by Tammy. Jean, Gwendolyn, Padma, Patience and Renee opened a free store on the waterfront and were written up in the paper. Arleane, Malgosia, Jennifer, Lara, Tara, Candace and Elisa collaborated on a community art project. And I, I gathered together the women remaining, Anar, Christabel, Naomi, Zoe, Yung Mi, Tracey, Michelle, Peggy, Monica and Leslie, and we planted a forest of flowers and bushes on the roof of our building.

We did not speak about the change, about why the

caretaker's disappearance lifted our moods. We never mentioned him at all.

Two months after he disappeared, I was wandering through the cavernous basement of our building, looking for a pail or container in which to carry soil (I had been gardening on the roof), when beside the furnace I noticed a door, like the door into my own apartment. The door was partly open and through it I saw a small apartment like my own and a bed. I pushed open the door and went right up to the bed where the caretaker was lying in the darkness, his chest rocking with laboured breaths. I asked him what was wrong. He sighed, as though resenting my intrusion, but told me.

Mould growing in the basement walls had infected his lungs, initiating a slow suffocation, his doctor believed. The caretaker's eyes were red and watery and the skin beneath his nostrils shone with mucous. Feeling something like pity, I reached forward to wipe at the mucous with my bare fingers.

He arched away from me, turning his face to the wall. "Don't. No don't!" he snapped, for the first time escaping his dignified manner in an effort to preserve it. His disgust with my action was apparent.

What I could not understand was that although he had lain sick and suffering, for days or weeks perhaps, his yellow shirt remained clean.

I left him lying with his face turned to the wall. I knew he would allow me no further ministrations, for the one thing he never gave was the chance to give in return. This weighed upon me. In accepting nothing from me on that day, he could not have taken more.

That Sunday at the laundromat, I decided to take up a collection for the caretaker. After depositing my contribution, I passed around a plastic laundry basket. When the basket returned to me, thirty-seven pennies lay in its bottom, as dull and brown as extinguished suns.

Acknowledgements

The dialogue spoken by authors in "Martin Amis Is in My Bed" was taken from passages in Martin Amis, *Money* (Penguin Books, 2000); Lorrie Moore, *Birds of America* (Picador USA, 1999); and Carol Shields, *Dressing Up for the Carnival* (Random House Canada, 2000).

With thanks to my mother for being my first and best editor, Nila Gupta for insightful reading and always knowing to ask twice how I was, Cynthia Holz and those who graced her workshops, Silas White for giving me permission to use scissors and Susan Banks, Jason Boyd, Dani Couture and Nathalie Foy for reassurance in the eleventh hour. I am also grateful for the financial support of the Toronto Arts Council, Ontario Arts Council and Canada Council for the Arts.